FEB 1 5

NOBODY WALKS

Books by Mick Herron

Down Cemetery Road
The Last Voice You Hear
Why We Die
Reconstruction
Smoke & Whispers
Nobody Walks

The Slough House Series
Slow Horses
Dead Lions

NOBODY
WALKS

Mick Herron

Published by Soho Press, Inc.
853 Broadway
New York, NY 10003

Library of Congress Cataloging-in-Publication Data

Herron, Mick.
Nobody walks / Mick Herron.

HC ISBN 978-1-61695-486-4
eISBN 978-1-61695-487-1

1. Great Britain. MI5—Officials and employees—Fiction. I. Title.
PR6108.E77N63 2014
823'.92—dc23
2014027671

Interior design by Janine Agro, Soho Press, Inc.

Printed in the United States of America

10 9 8 7 6 5 4 3 2 1

To Tony and Christine

PART ONE

■   ■   ■

1.1

The news had come hundreds of miles to sit waiting for days in a mislaid phone. And there it lingered like a moth in a box, weightless, and aching for the light.

The street cleaners' lorry woke Bettany. It was 4:25 A.M. He washed at the sink, dressed, turned the bed's thin mattress, and rolled his sleeping bag into a tight package he leaned upright in a corner. 4:32.

Locking the door was an act of faith or satire—the lock would barely withstand a rattle—but the room wouldn't be empty long, because someone else used it during the day. Bettany hadn't met him, but they'd reached an accommodation. The daytime occupant respected Bettany's possessions—his toothbrush, his sleeping bag, the dog-eared copy of *Dubliners* he'd found on a bus—and in return Bettany left untouched the clothing that hung from a hook on the door, three shirts and a pair of khakis.

His own spare clothing he kept in a duffel bag in a locker at the sheds. Passport and wallet he carried in a security belt with his mobile, until that got lost or stolen.

Outside was February cold, quiet enough that he could hear water rinsing the sewers. A bus grumbled past, windows fogged. Bettany nodded to the whore on the corner, whose territory was bounded by two streetlights. She was Senegalese, pre-op, currently a redhead, and he'd bought her a drink one night, God knew why. They had exile in common, but little else. Bettany's French remained undistinguished, and the hooker's English didn't lend itself to small talk.

A taste of the sea hung in the air. This would burn off later, and be replaced by urban flavours.

He caught the next bus, a twenty-minute ride to the top of a lane which fell from the main road like an afterthought, and as he trudged downhill a truck passed, horn blaring, its headlights yellowing the sheds ahead, which were barn-sized constructions behind wire-topped fences. A wooden sign hung lopsided from the gates, one of its tethering chains longer than the other. The words were faded by weather. Bettany had never been able to make them out.

Audible now, the sound of cattle in distress.

He was waved through and fetched his apron from the locker room. A group of men were smoking by the door, and one grunted his name.

"Tonton."

What they called him, for reasons lost in the mist of months.

He knotted his apron, which was stained so thick with blood and grease it felt plastic, and fumbled his gloves on.

Out in the yard the truck was impatient, its exhaust fumes spoiling out in thick black ropes. The noise from the nearest shed was mechanical, mostly, and its smells metallic and full of fear. Behind Bettany men stamped their cigarettes out and hawked noisily. Refrigerated air whispered from the truck's dropped tailgate.

Bettany's role wasn't complicated. Lorries arrived bearing cattle and the cattle were fed into the sheds. What came out was meat, which was then ferried away in different lorries. Bettany's job, and that of his companions, was to carry the meat to the lorries. This not only required no thought, it demanded thought's absence.

At day's end he'd hose down the yard, a task he performed with grim diligence, meticulously blasting every scrap of matter down the drains.

He switched off, and the working day took over. This was measured in a familiar series of aches and smells and sounds, the same actions repeated with minor variations, while blurred memories nagged him uninvited, moments which had seemed unexceptional at the time, but had persisted. A woman in a café, regarding him with what might have been interest, might have been contempt. An evening at the track with Majeed, who was the nearest he'd made to a friend, though he hadn't made enemies. He didn't think he'd made enemies.

Thoughts became rituals in themselves. You plodded the same course over and over, like any dumb beast or wind-up toy.

At about the time citizens would be leaving their homes in clean shirts Bettany stopped for coffee, pitch black in a polystyrene cup. He ate a hunk of bread wrapped round cheese, leaning against the fence and watching grey weather arrive, heading inland.

From three metres' distance Majeed detached himself from a group similarly occupied.

"Hey, Tonton. You lose your mobile?"

It spun through the air. He caught it one-handed.

"*Ou?*"

"*La Girondelle.*"

The bar at the track. He was surprised to see it again, though the reason why wasn't long in coming.

"*C'est de la merde.* Not worth stealing."

Bettany gave no argument.

The piece of shit, not worth stealing, was barely worth ringing either, though still had a flicker of charge. Four missed calls in nine days. Two were local numbers and hadn't left messages. The others were from England, unfamiliar streams of digits. Odds were they were cold calls, checking out his inclinations vis-à-vis internet banking or double-glazing. He finished his coffee undecided whether to listen or delete, then found his thumb resolving the issue of its own accord, scrolling to his voicemail number, pressing play.

"Yes, this is Detective Sergeant Welles, speaking from Hoxton police station. Er, London. I'm trying to reach a Mr. Thomas Bettany? If you could give me a ring at your earliest convenience. It's a matter of some importance." He recited a number slowly enough that Bettany caught it the first time.

His mouth was dry. The bread, the cheese, grew lumpy in his stomach.

The second voice was less measured.

"Mr. Bettany? Liam's father?" It was a girl, or young woman. "My name's Flea, Felicity Pointer? I'm calling about Liam . . . Mr. Bettany, I'm so sorry to have to tell you this."

She sounded sorry.

"There's been an accident. Liam—I'm sorry, Mr. Bettany. Liam died."

Either she paused a long while or the recorded silence dragged itself out in slow motion, eating up his pre-paid minutes.

"I'm sorry."

"Message ends. To hear the message envelope, press one. To save the—"

He killed the robot voice.

Nearby, Majeed was halfway through a story, dropping into English when French wasn't obscene enough. Bettany could hear the creaking of a trolley's metal wheels, a chain scraping over a beam. Another lorry trundled down the lane, its grille broad, an American model. Already details were stacking up. More blurred snapshots he'd flick through in future days, always associated with the news just heard.

He reached for the back of his neck, and untied his apron.

"Tonton?"

He dropped it to the ground.

"*Ou vas-tu?*"

Bettany fetched his duffel from the locker.

1.2

The crematorium was single-storey, stucco-clad, with a high chimney. On one side creeping plants swarmed a cane trellis that bordered an array of small gardens divided by hedges. Japanese stones neighboured ornamental ponds and bonsai trees peered from terracotta pots. Other patches echoed formal English styles, orchards, terraced rosebeds, in any of which you might strew the ashes of the departed, supposing the deceased had expressed a preference.

Bettany imagined Liam saying, *When I'm dead, scatter me on a Japanese garden. Not in actual Japan. Just anywhere handy.*

A mild English winter was turning chill, but all that remained of the morning's frost was a damp smudge on the pavements. The imprints of vanished leaves were stamped there too, like the work of a graffiti artist who'd run out of things to say.

Bettany's once-blond shaggy hair was now streaked grey, like his ragged beard, and while his eyes were strikingly blue, their expression was vague. His hands, large and raw, were jammed in the pockets of a cheap raincoat, and he rocked slightly on feet cased in work boots that had seen better days. Under the coat he wore jeans, a long-sleeved crew-neck tee and a zippered top. These were the spare clothes from his duffel bag, but three days' wear had taken their toll. The duffel itself he'd abandoned in a bin, he couldn't remember which side of the Channel. For all the hours he'd spent on buses, he'd managed little sleep. His only conversation had been a brief exchange on the ferry, when a French trucker lent him the use of a phone charger.

His first stop on reaching London had been Hoxton Police Station.

Detective Sergeant Welles, once located, had been sympathetic.

"I'm sorry for your loss."

Bettany nodded.

"Nobody seemed to know where you were. But there was an idea you were out of the country. I'm glad you got back in time."

Which was how he discovered the cremation was taking place that morning.

He'd sat in the back row. The chapel of remembrance was quarter-full, most of the congregation Liam's age, none of them known to him, but an introduction contained a familiar name, Felicity Pointer. Flea, she'd called herself on the phone. She approached the lectern looking twenty-five, twenty-six, brunette and lightly olive-skinned, wearing black of course. Hardly looking at the assembled company, she read a short poem about chimney sweeps, then returned to her seat.

Watching this, Bettany had barely paid attention to the main object of interest, but looking at it now he realised that what he'd been feeling these past three days was not grief but numbness. A pair of curtains provided the backdrop, and behind them the coffin would soon pass, and there the remains of his only son would be reduced to ash and fragments of bone, to the mess of clinker you'd find in a grate on a winter's morning. Nothing of substance. And all Bettany could make of it was an all-consuming absence of feeling, as if he was indeed the stranger his son had made of him.

He rose and slipped out of the door.

Waiting by the trellis, it struck him that it was seven years since he'd been in London. He supposed he ought to be noticing differences, things being better or worse, but he couldn't see much had changed. The skyline had altered, with new towers jutting heavenwards from the City, and more poised to sprout everywhere you looked. But that had always been the case. London had never been finished, and never would be. Or not by dint of new construction.

Seven years since London, three of them in Lyme. Then Hannah had died, and he'd left England. Now Liam had died, and he was back.

Welles had given him a lift here. There might have been a hidden agenda, pump the father for information, but Bettany had none to offer and the flow had gone the other way. How it had happened, for instance. Up through France, across the choppy Channel, Bettany hadn't known the how. Of the various possibilities some kind of traffic accident had seemed most likely, Liam driving too fast on a fog-bound stretch of motorway, or a bus mounting the pavement, Liam in the wrong place. He could have called and spared himself conjecture, but that would have been to make imagination fact. Now he learned that there had been no cars involved, no buses. Liam had fallen from the window of his flat.

"Were you in close contact with your son, Mr. Bettany?"

"No."

"So you wouldn't know much about his lifestyle?"

"I don't even know where he lived."

"Not far from here."

Which would make it N1. Not somewhere Bettany was familiar with. He gathered it was trendy, if that word was used any more, and if it wasn't, well then. Cool. Hip. Whatever.

Had Liam been hip? he wondered. Had Liam been cool? They hadn't spoken in four years. He couldn't swear to any aspect of his late son's life, down to the most basic details. Had he been gay? Vegetarian? A biker? What did he do at weekends, browse secondhand shops, looking for bargain furniture? Or hang around the clubs, looking to score? Bettany didn't know. And while he could find out, that wouldn't erase the indelible truth of this particular moment, the one he spent outside the chapel where Liam's body was being fed into the flames. Here and now, he knew nothing. And still, somehow, felt less.

Overhead, a stringy scrap of smoke loosed itself from the chimney. Then another. And now here came the rest of it, billowing and scattering, a cloud for only a moment, and then nothing, and nowhere, ever again.

1.3

The chapel had both entrance and exit, and fresh mourners were congregating at the former. Leaving them, Bettany wandered round to the back, where those who'd come for Liam were dispersing. He was the only blood relative here—there were no others. Liam, an only child, had been the son of only children. And his mother was four years dead.

Loitering under a tree, he watched Flea Pointer emerge. She was talking to an older man, himself flanked by another—flanked, as if the second man were a minder or subordinate. The first man was mid-thirties or so, and while dark suits were the order of the day his seemed of a different cut, the cloth darker, the shirt whiter. A matter of money, Bettany supposed. His short hair was fair to the point of translucence, and his wire-framed glasses tinted blue. As Bettany watched Pointer leaned forward and kissed him on the cheek, her arm curling round his back for a moment, and the man tensed. He raised his hand as if to pat her on the back, but thought better of it. Releasing him, she brushed a palm across her eyes, sweeping her hair free or dabbing at tears. They exchanged inaudible words and the men moved off, down the path, through the gate into the street, and disappeared inside a long silver car, which pulled off with barely a noise. Flea Pointer still hadn't moved.

She was the same age as Liam had been, though unlike Liam was petite—Liam had been a tall boy, gangly, with arms and legs too spindly to know where their centre of balance lay. He'd filled as he'd grown, and had maybe kept doing so. He might have barrelled out since then. Bettany didn't know.

As he stood thinking such things, the girl looked round and saw him.

Flea Pointer watched Vincent Driscoll climb into the limo and pull away, Boo Berryman driving. She had felt him flinch when she put her arm round him—Vincent wasn't much for human contact. She had forgotten that in the emotion of the moment, or else had thought that he might forget it in that same emotion. But he hadn't, so he'd flinched, and she was left feeling gauche and adolescent, as if there weren't enough feelings washing around her now. Tears were not far away. The world threatened to blur.

But she blinked, and it shimmied back. When vision cleared, she was looking at a man standing under a tree like a figure in a fable. He was tall, bearded, shaggy-haired, inappropriately dressed, and she wasn't sure which of these details clinched it, but she knew he was Liam's father. With that knowledge slotted in place, she approached him.

"Mr. Bettany?"

He nodded.

"I'm Flea—"

"I know."

He sounded brusque, but why wouldn't he? His son had just

been cremated. The emotion of the moment, again. She knew this could take different forms.

On the other hand, he'd never responded to her phone call. She'd dug his number out from a form at work, Liam's next-of-kin contact. Couldn't recall exactly what she'd said. But he'd never called back.

What he said now, though, was, "You rang me. Thank you."

"You live abroad."

This sounded disjointed even to her own ears.

"Liam told me," she added.

How else would she have known? She was coming adrift from this exchange already.

"I'm so sorry, I hated to tell you like that, but I didn't know what else to do—"

"You did the right thing."

"I know you hadn't been getting on. I mean, Liam said you didn't—hadn't—"

"We hadn't been in touch," Bettany said.

His gaze left hers to focus on something behind her. Without meaning to, she turned. A small group, three men, one woman, still lingered by the chapel door, but even as she registered this they began to move off. Instead of heading for the gate they walked round to the front, as if heading back inside. One of the men was carrying something. It took Flea a moment to recognise it as a thermos flask.

Liam's father asked her, "Who was that you were talking to?"

"When?"

"He just left."

"Oh . . . That was Vincent. Vincent Driscoll?"

It was clear he didn't know who Vincent Driscoll was.

"We worked for him. Liam and I did. Well, I still do."

She bit her lip. Tenses were awkward, in the company of the bereaved. Apologies had to be implied, for the offence of still living.

"So you were colleagues," he said. "Doing what?"

"Vincent's a game designer. *Shades?*"

Bettany nodded, but she could tell the name meant nothing. Distantly, music swelled. The next service was starting. Flea Pointer had the sudden understanding that life was a conveyor belt, a slow rolling progress to the dropping-off point, and that once you'd fallen you'd be followed by the next in line. An unhappy thought, which could be shrugged off anywhere but here.

If Tom Bettany was having similar thoughts you wouldn't know it from his expression. He seemed just barely involved in what had happened here this morning.

"Thank you," he said again, and left. Flea watched as he headed down the path.

He didn't look back.

1.4

In the car leaving the crematorium Vincent Driscoll felt one of his headaches coming on, a designation his late mother had coined to distinguish Vincent's headaches from anyone else's. It seemed to fit. There was no denying whose headache this was. It felt like a bubble was squeezing its way through his brain.

He found his Ibuprofen, dry-swallowed a pair, and asked Boo to drive more slowly, or thought he did, and sank back. Had he actually spoken? The world through his tinted glasses, edges softened, passed by at the same speed.

Left to his own devices, he'd have avoided the service. He hated gatherings, and this one had changed nothing. Liam Bettany remained dead. Which was the kind of thing he mostly remembered not to say aloud, but there was no rule he couldn't think it. Probably everyone had thoughts like that, the whole notion of "polite society" being little more than a hedge against honesty. Normality was rarely what it appeared. This much Vincent knew.

And this time, he definitely spoke out loud. "Boo? Could you . . ."

He mimed a movement, a gesture with no obvious correlation to any of the actions involved in driving a car, but which Boo Berryman, watching in the rearview mirror, interpreted correctly. He slowed down. Vincent closed his eyes.

A succession of pastel-coloured characters drifted past, walking down perfectly straight streets, lined with traditional shops. Each was armed with a shopping list, and carried a basket under an arm, and each popped into every shop in turn, in a perfectly choreographed retail ballet . . . A round yellow sun rose and fell in the sky behind them.

Vincent, who had dreamt up *Shades* when he was twelve, sometimes wondered how many others there were who could ascribe their entire life story to one moment, one striking thought. Einstein, perhaps. Maybe Douglas Adams. Anyway. He'd been playing Tetris, in that semi-catatonic way it induced, when he'd had the sudden sense of things having flipped—that he was the game, not the player.

That had been the spark. Everything else had taken years. But years were what he had had, this being an advantage of having your big idea young.

The car purred to a halt. Traffic lights. Various noises, muffled by thick windows, sprayed past as if fired from a shotgun. Heavy beats and pitched whistling. Sounds of metal and rubber, of the forces that drove everything. If he had ever found a form of music he enjoyed, this was when he would listen to it . . .

Shades had started small, in the sense that it was a one-man show. The team he had now, marketing and packaging and all the rest—he'd had nobody then. Design had happened in his bedroom. Production, outsourced piecemeal to half a dozen tiny companies, had swallowed every penny of his mother's legacy. The result resembled an arcade giveaway, a game fated to be bundled up with others and sold as a lucky dip. Even the small independent he'd hired to mastermind distribution tried to talk him down. The number of titles coming onto the market, if you didn't get traction in the first quarter, you were history. He'd be better off using it on a CV, blagging his way into a job with one of the big boys. But he'd insisted on going ahead.

And it had started small, too, in the sense that not many people bought it. Turned on its head, though—the way Vincent liked to look at things—what this meant was, it was bought only by those who bought everything, which was fine by him. A steady trickle diminishing to a drip, but fine by him. Because, monitoring the comment boards, Vincent knew nobody had cracked it. If that happened and the trickle remained a trickle, he'd know he'd failed. But until then, everyone else had.

Besides, Vincent knew gamers. Gamers were essentially kids, and didn't throw games away. They swapped them and left them gathering dust and stacked them in towers twenty jewelcases high, but they didn't throw them away because that was an adult trait. And games that didn't get thrown away eventually got played again, once they were old enough to have regained novelty value.

The big danger was the format would become extinct, and that had given him a bad night or two, had tempted him to nudge events himself, and post his own message.

But not long after the game's first birthday, everything changed.

Vincent picked it up on a gamers' board.

anyone cracked Shades?

When he'd read this, something shifted inside him.

Home. Sometimes Vincent waited for Boo to open the door, but today he was out of the car before the electronic gates whumped shut. In the kitchen he ran the tap to make sure the water was cold, then filled a glass. This he drained without turning the tap off. He filled a second, and drank that too. Then a third. His headache decreased to a background grumble. He filled a fourth glass and carried it back into the sitting room, which covered most of the ground floor. Boo was just coming in, and flashed him a concerned look. Vincent shook his head, meaning leave him alone. Boo carried straight on into the kitchen, where Vincent heard him turn the tap off. Vincent loosened his tie and sank into a chair.

Above another sofa was a picture, seven foot by four, of a cartoon dog. Some cartoon dogs look intelligent, others dim or violent. Some manage sexy. This one pulled off the relatively simple trick of being nondescript, an expressionless brown mongrel, captured in the act of walking against a two-tone background, the lower half grey, the upper yellow. Those who knew the dog recognised these shades for what they were, which was pavement and wall. And nobody who didn't know the dog had ever seen the picture, so alternative interpretations had never been offered.

follow the dog

That had been the clue offered by that first gamer, the one who'd "cracked" *Shades*. By the time Vincent had revisited the board, it was in meltdown.

holy shit

that is awsum!

way!!!

Shades had been written off by serious gamers, as Vincent had expected. They demanded high-spec graphics, way beyond his budget at the time, and this was just another kitsch time-passer, whose animated figures echoed BBC kids' programming from the '80s, all big heads and fixed smiles, wandering round in a

Truman Show–like daze, collecting shopping. It was a speed-trial, in which the player had to gather the various items on a list faster than the game-generated characters managed. If you changed the order in which you visited the shops, you could shave seconds off your total, but ran the risk that by the time you got to, say, the butcher's, he'd be out of sausages. There was—so the rules governing such games dictated—a perfect schematic, if the player could only discover it, one which took into account all the other characters' purchases, and the order in which they did things. These days, it might be one of fifty games stored on a phone, something to while away a journey. Even then it was nothing special, a different league from the Lara Crofts, the FPSs.

Nothing special unless you followed the dog.

The dog was a jerky-looking mutt, and if you played the game four times on the trot it appeared briefly on the main street, ambled round a corner and up an alley, and paused halfway to piss on a lamp post. Most players who'd stuck that far had assumed that was it, a little reward for persistence. An animated dog taking a cartoon piss. After which it trotted round another corner and out of sight.

But if, instead of heading into a shop to collect the next item on the list, you followed the dog round that corner, and kept on following it until it dug its way under a bush on a scrappy piece of wasteland which didn't appear to have been there until that moment—because it hadn't, in fact, been there until that moment—and scrabbled down the resulting hole after it, well, once you'd done that, you were in a whole new world.

Raising his glass to his lips, Vincent discovered it empty. He'd drained it without noticing. Still thirsty, though. But perhaps that was unsurprising, given that he'd spent the morning watching a coffin being fed into the flames—which couldn't actually be seen, but was impossible to ignore. The wooden box, with its unnecessarily plush interior, sliding into an oven, never to come out. The smoke drifting into the sky . . . Another gateway, he thought. A chimney instead of a hole, but still, another gateway into a new world.

And Liam Bettany discovering this one now, just as he'd discovered the other.

anyone cracked Shades?

Liam had been the first to follow the dog. In a way Vincent owed him everything, which had never occurred to him until this moment. It wasn't an important thought, but felt similar enough to grief that he savoured it a while—tended it, to see if it would grow—and even when it didn't, held on to it a little longer, carrying it back into the kitchen, where he poured another glass of water while Boo prepared a late lunch.

1.5

The policeman had told him where Liam had lived, a rented third-floor flat, and Bettany had memorised the address but had no idea where it was. He stopped at the first shop he came to and asked the woman behind the counter for help. It wasn't far. She gave efficient directions.

He'd have bought something from her but only had euros, and not many, forty or so. Maybe thirty quid, enough to feed himself at least. He hadn't eaten in how long? Memory suggested a fast-chicken franchise on the ferry, and alongside this image sat another, of oil-flecked water, and big-winged gulls on the watch for spilled food.

The address was one of a terraced row twelve houses long on a quiet street. The row was brick, and the upper windows boasted wrought-iron railings wrapped around ledges no wider than shelves. Greenery sprouted in pots from some, and he could make out a bird feeder on one, small pouches of nuts hanging from its curling branches.

It was accidental. He fell from the balcony, kind of balcony, of his flat.

The windowframes were uniformly white, as if in response to some local mandate, but the doors were vari-coloured, blues, reds, greens and purples. The door of Liam's building was red.

Bettany rang the bell.

The landlord's name was Greenleaf, and the ground floor was where he lived. He was a thin, needy-looking man in plaid shirt and baggy trousers, his eyes set far back in his head. On learning Bettany's name he wrinkled with suspicion, as if Bettany were responsible for the aggravation involved in having a fatal accident on the premises.

"I knew nothing about any of this drug-taking," he said.

"I'd like the key."

"It's in the lease. No illegal substances on the premises."

"Noted. The key?"

"What do you want it for?"

Bettany said, "I'm going to collect my son's possessions. Do you have a problem with that?"

He didn't think he'd leaned on this especially, but Greenleaf stepped back.

"No need to get aggressive."

He left Bettany hanging in the hall while he disappeared behind a door, emerging at length with a key on a string.

"How long will you be?"

There was maybe a joke there, relating to the piece of string, but Bettany couldn't summon up the interest. Without replying, he took the key and carried on up the stairs.

Was he drunk?

He'd been drinking.

Drugs?

We think that's why he was out on the balcony. Kind of balcony.

The top-floor landing was graced with a skylight, through

which grey light fell like drizzle. There was a door on either side. Liam's opened, with his key, onto a small hallway, into which similar light fell from a companion skylight, this one blazoned with a streak of bird shit. The walls were white and the carpet beige, a little scuffed. The air was stale, but Bettany had known worse.

There were three rooms off the hallway. The first was a cupboard-sized bathroom without a bath, just sink, shower and toilet. The cabinet above the sink was mirrored, and Bettany opened it as much to avoid his reflection as out of curiosity about what it held. Which was the usual. Razor, soap, deodorant, a fresh tube of toothpaste. A bottle of bleach sat next to the toilet, tucked behind the loo brush. The shower was clean, with just the odd speck of mould eating into the grouting. A small print on the wall showed a boat bobbing on an unconvincing sea.

Across the hall was the kitchen, which wasn't much bigger but had room for oven, fridge, sink, washing machine, and overhead cupboards neatly filled with essentials. Tins of pulses, bags of rice, flour, jars of sauces. On a white plastic sink-tidy, a single plate had long since dried itself.

Among the postcards stuck to the fridge was a photo of Hannah from before she grew sick. Unthinkingly he pulled it free for a closer look. But it was no riddle awaiting solution. It was an old photograph, that was all.

The fridge obligingly carried on humming, keeping up the good work of chilling Liam's out-of-date milk and slowly perishing vegetables. An array of bowls, sealed with clingfilm, held leftovers he'd never finish. It was all very clean, Bettany thought. All surfaces wiped. Cutlery in its drawer. Pans in their cupboard, graded by size.

Liam had always been careful about his possessions. Very neat in his arrangements.

Detective Sergeant Welles had told him, "There were effects, odds and ends. What he had in his pockets, I mean."

What he had in his pockets when he'd hit the ground.

"You can collect them from the station. Or . . . Where are you staying, can I ask, sir? You've come from abroad, that right?"

Bettany had said, "I'm not sure yet. Where I'm staying."

The other door led into the living room, which would be a nice bright space on a sunny day, with those big windows. A sofa was set against one wall, alongside a nearly full bookcase. On a low table was an electrical contrivance which Bettany guessed was a music system, and a surprisingly small TV set. A rubber plant, scraping the ceiling, lived between the windows, and a small writing desk with a chair occupied a corner. On it was a flat white laptop with the Apple logo.

Another doorway in the far wall presumably led to the bedroom. Bettany checked. Bed, wardrobe and chest of drawers with a mirror propped on top. The bed was made. A small window looked out on the backs of other, similar houses. Below it was a wooden chair, on which lay a folded pair of jeans.

He returned to the sitting room, with its big windows, which didn't quite reach to the floor.

Sort of balcony?

It's just a ledge. A ledge with a railing, meant for putting plants on, so people in upstairs flats can enjoy a bit of garden. What it's not meant for is smoking a joint on. Because there's not much room for being straight, let alone getting high.

The nearest window had a small security lock. Bettany unscrewed it, released the latch, and heaved the window up as high as it would go. The air that blustered in was cold. Down below, a car was inching into a parking space only marginally larger than itself.

Easing himself through, he stepped onto the balcony not meant for getting high on. It was no more than a foot wide, with a terracotta pot on either end, a dead plant in each. Between the two you could stand, if you were careful, leaning on the brickwork for support. It wasn't somewhere you could grow too comfortable, unless, Bettany supposed, you were young and immortal. When you were young, you could fly, or at least bounce. That was the theory, anyway.

He checked the pot to his left, then made a similar examination of the one on his right. Neither had been used as an ashtray.

This was a pretty strong blend. There's a lot of it around lately. They're calling it muskrat. Well, they'd already used skunk.

Muskrat. Bettany closed his eyes, and imagined the seamless sequence, Liam rolling up, stepping through the window, lighting a joint, and then—what? Losing his balance? Closing his eyes, forgetting where he was? It must have been strong stuff all right. First you get high. Then you come crashing down.

After giving that a little more thought, he climbed back inside.

1.6

Pulling the window shut, Bettany noticed he still held Hannah's photograph. He took it back to the kitchen and reclamped it to the fridge, then had to lean against the wall while a wave of tiredness struck. He needed coffee. Shouldn't be too difficult to manage.

A cafetière sat by the kettle and there was coffee in the fridge. Bettany boiled the kettle, and while the coffee drew, went through cupboards again. Tins, bags of rice and jars of spices. A memory was stirring, but it wasn't until he saw the matching plastic containers marked TEA, BISCUITS, SUGAR that he knew what it was. Reaching for the third container he unscrewed its lid. It held sugar, sure enough, but when he dipped his fingers through its temporary glaze they met a polythene bag, the kind banks use for change, rolled into a tight cylinder. Unwrapping it, Bettany counted out two hundred and forty pounds in twenties.

He weighed it in his hand. The sugar tin was where Hannah had hidden small sums of cash. Bettany used to shake his head— the sugar tin? Please. But that's where she'd kept her emergency fund, and where Liam had kept his too. Bettany shook his head

again, less at the way things were handed down, and more at
the fact that the police hadn't found it. They must have been
through the flat looking for drugs, if nothing else. Muskrat.
Who thought up these names?

The coffee was ready. He poured a cup, left it black, carried
it into the sitting room. Taking his raincoat off at last, he draped it
over the sofa, then opened Liam's laptop. It swam into life without complaint but asked for a password. After pondering this for
a while, Bettany closed the lid.

A yawn caught him unawares. He hadn't slept in—he couldn't
bring himself to perform the calculation. Too many hours. He
hadn't slept in too many hours. The coffee would help.

When the phone rang he at first didn't realise it was his own,
and once he had it took him a moment to locate it. It was in his
raincoat pocket, and before he'd retrieved it, the ringing stopped.
But in moving the coat, or else putting his weight on the sofa's
cushions, he'd released an aroma that hadn't been there before. It
wasn't much, a fading scent, but it caught him where he lived,
raising hairs at the back of his neck. It was the smell of his son.
The ordinary, living smell of Liam, of his soap, and his sweat, and
of oils that had seeped from his hair as he sat here, head against
the cushions.

The phone rang again.

"Mr. Bettany?"

He didn't reply.

"Mr.—?"

"Yes."

"It's DS Welles, sir. You're at your son's flat, are you?"

"Yes."

"I have his things. His effects."

Effects was a policeman's word.

"And I'm just outside. Should I—"

"I'll come down."

He waited two minutes, then did so. Welles was on the step, offering a brown envelope that might have come from the Revenue, or anywhere else that issued impersonal demands. Bettany took it in his left hand. His right was jammed in his pocket.

"Thanks."

"Are you going to be all right?"

"I expect so."

"Is there anyone—"

"I'll be all right."

"Of course. Here, I need you to sign this, sir."

Bettany scrawled his name on the proffered form, *I hereby acknowledge receipt*, and turned back inside. Before shutting the door he said, "How did you know I was here?"

"Couldn't think where else you'd be."

Upstairs, he turned the envelope over. Objects inside it slipped from side to side. Eventually he ripped the seal and poured its contents onto the table.

A wallet, holding a little over thirty pounds, two credit cards, a supermarket loyalty card and a library ticket.

A set of doorkeys.

A chapstick.

A packet of tissues.

That was it.

He dumped everything on the desk next to the laptop and finished his coffee. Knowing it wasn't a great idea, that it would give him the jitters, he poured a second cup anyway, drained it, and poured a third. That was the end of the coffee. He wandered the flat again, cup in hand. Everywhere was clean lines, clutter-free surfaces. A thin layer of dust was forming, exactly measurable,

Bettany thought, to the day of his son's death. There were no candles melting into wax-smeared holders, no knick-knacks acquired on holiday to forever take up space. No photographs, other than those on the fridge.

None of which were of Bettany.

He wouldn't have expected any. He was surprised Liam had listed his number as an emergency contact—wouldn't have been shocked to learn he was passing as an orphan. As Bettany recalled it, that had been the import of their last conversation.

It's your fault she's dead.

It's cancer's fault, Liam.

And why do you think people get cancer? You made her unhappy. You were a bastard to her, and to me.

There was a whole deluded industry dedicated to the notion that cancer fattened on the emotions, and not for a moment had Bettany believed his son had fallen prey to it. It had been a weapon, that's all. A stick to beat him with.

Had he been a bastard? He'd been called worse.

One of the pictures of Liam was recent, taken indoors. His hair, always darker than his father's, was cut short, and he wore a white collarless shirt, open at the neck. Half-smiling, half-serious, he seemed to be trying to impress the photographer with both sides of his personality. Twenty-six years old. Bettany unclipped it and carried it into the other room.

On the sofa he closed his eyes, photo on his chest. It was quiet. Caffeinated to the eyeballs, he didn't expect to sleep but drifted anyway, memories of a much younger Liam overlapping with those of Hannah, distant snapshots that offered no clue to how badly things would go awry. *It's your fault she's dead.* There was no way in the world those words were true, and no way to unremember them.

The light through the windows had weakened when he stood and put his raincoat on. Leaving the flat, he went downstairs. When Greenleaf opened the door he was holding a paper napkin, wiping his mouth. He'd missed a fleck of grease that shone on his chin.

"Did you bring the key back?" he said.

"When was the rent paid up to?"

"I can't remember offhand." Greenleaf's eyes glazed, as if he were engaged in a mental calculation he'd hoped would be overlooked. "I could work it out, refund the balance. Leave your address and I'll post you a cheque."

"No need," Bettany said. "I'll be upstairs. Until the rent's used up."

He didn't wait for a response. Outside, he stood for a while by the patch of road where Liam's life had ended. Nothing distinguished that space from any other. It was just where something had happened. Looking up at the building offered no stories either. Everything carried on doing what it had always done. Bettany put his hands in his pockets, and went walking.

1.7

Flea Pointer had a problem, a problem the size of a box, which was precisely what it was. Inside the box was an urn, squatter and rounder than she might have imagined, and inside the urn was Liam Bettany.

In life, Liam had been tall, limby—not a real word but his limbs had been noticeably long, his hands dangling lower than seemed plausible, his legs an obstacle in the workplace. As days wore on he'd sink lower and lower into his chair, allowing them to protrude further and further, and more than once, passing his desk, she'd nearly gone flat on her face. His response was always an apologetic grin.

She'd never really tripped, though. Never fallen.

Flea was in her studio flat in a canalside development near the Angel. Better apartments had more rooms and overlooked the lock, but Flea wasn't complaining. Before this there'd been a series of house shares, most of which had degenerated into attritional warfare, the battlegrounds being bathroom and kitchen, and whose stuff was whose. She'd seen violence break out over a pint of milk. Now, when the walls felt like they were closing in, she heaved a sigh of relief they were closing on her alone.

Not quite alone at the moment, though. Liam was here too.

Her colleagues had taken off to a pub once the service was over, and were presumably still there, toasting Liam and celebrating small memories of him, like her own recollection of his troublesome legs. She had joined them for an hour before returning to the crem to take possession of the ashes, which she'd half-expected Vincent to do, though on reflection wasn't sure why. Vincent had taken care of expenses, but he'd never realistically been likely to step higher than that. So here she was, and here Liam was too, in a box on her table, her friend.

There'd been a time when they might have been more than friends, but in the end—or before the beginning—Flea had decided this was a bad idea. So now, instead of memories of a romantic interlude, she was left thinking about his long legs, and how they stuck out too far, and could easily have caused an accident.

Which evidently they had done, if not to her. She knew that ledge outside his window, with its low railing that came halfway up his calves. No wonder he'd gone over. If she'd been with him last week—and it wouldn't have been the first time they'd sat out there together, getting high—she might have saved him.

On the other hand she might have been left sitting stoned on the balcony, looking down at his body, knowing her life was as irrevocably twisted, as bent out of shape, as he was . . .

Flea Pointer shook her head. Dreadful imaginings. And utterly selfish at their root, which she didn't mean to be, not today. Not with Liam gone.

She'd miss his grin.

She cried again.

■   ■   ■

Afterwards, tears dry, the problem endured. Liam's ashes remained on her coffee table, and fond as she'd been of him she didn't want him as a roommate, even if arguments about the milk weren't likely to arise.

The answer, of course, was staring her in the face. It was simply a matter of deciding whether it meant being disloyal to Liam. Seeing Tom Bettany at the service had been a surprise. Because he hadn't responded she'd assumed he'd not received her message, or had no intention of acting on it. Liam would have professed to believe the latter. When in full flow about his father—a man he insisted he didn't like talking about—he'd revealed more than he intended, but given that on such occasions he was usually a little drunk or a little high, this was not unusual. Given that Flea too had tended to be one or the other, she couldn't pretend total recall. But they hadn't got on, that was an understatement. Liam had coloured their estrangement in Shakespearean terms, once claiming his father had killed his mother. That moment Flea did recall clearly, along with its pale-faced aftermath, when Liam threw up, luckily in the bathroom, then shakily admitted he'd exaggerated, that it hadn't been an actual killing so much as . . .

And she remembered that too. The way he'd lacked words to state the case. Because, she suspected, when it came down to it, he'd been a boy who'd lost his mother too young, and needed someone to blame. His father fit the bill, that was all. The murder claim, like others he'd made, Flea put down to immaturity. And the fact that his father's number was on his contact list at work indicated that at some level he'd known it too. Had understood there'd come a time when a bridge would need rebuilding.

Too late for that now.

Still grieving, still pained, Flea couldn't deny she was also curious. Though she'd had no mental picture of Liam's father, it nevertheless surprised her that he resembled a tramp, with shaggy hair and scarecrow's beard, and clothes he'd been wearing a while. And, too, the wariness she'd noticed in homeless people. The way he'd checked out the crowd at the chapel, as if weighing potential threat. But he remained Liam's father, the rightful owner of his son's remains. Presenting him with them wouldn't be an act of disloyalty to Liam but the opposite. And as much of a bridge as either could now hope for.

The solution, then, was a phone call away, but still Flea Pointer hesitated. She had no idea where Bettany was. Perhaps he'd already made tracks, was already standing at a motorway slip road, thumb in the air . . . She didn't know why that image came to mind. He didn't look the type to ask favours of strangers. Which meant he wouldn't want them done unawares, she decided, and that conclusion reached, she looked for her mobile. Do it now. Do it now, and it was done. Her phone was in her bag. She made the call before second thoughts could persuade her otherwise.

1.8

Bettany's walk had carried him three streets away to a pub with green doors and the promise of live music, though thankfully not right then. He bought a Guinness and a whisky chaser, paying for both from Liam's stash. His son, buying him a drink. Two drinks. That gave him pause as he raised the Guinness to his lips.

He didn't have a lot of time to dwell on it because his mobile rang.

Unknown caller, but it was Flea Pointer.

"Mr. Bettany?"

Who else would be answering his phone?

"How are you? I mean, are you . . ."

He got the impression she hadn't planned this call.

"I'm fine," he said.

He picked up his shot glass and held it to the light.

"I just—Mr. Bettany, I've got Liam here. Sorry, that was stupid. Liam's ashes. I have Liam's ashes."

He didn't reply.

"I didn't know you were going to be there, so when we made the arrangements, I said I'd take them . . ."

He'd stood watching ribbons of smoke being torn from the chimney, and it hadn't occurred to him to collect the ashes. What else had he missed?

"Mr. Bettany?"

He cleared his throat. "I heard."

"So . . . well, if you want to collect them, or let me know where you are, I could bring them to you. If you want me to."

"I don't know where I am."

"I'm not . . ."

"I'm in a pub near Liam's. A green pub."

Pause.

"Yeah, no, I know the one you mean. Look, give me ten minutes? I'll join you."

She seemed to expect a response so Bettany said, "I'm not going anywhere," and ended the call.

It was more like twenty, and Bettany was on his second pair of drinks. The pub remained half-empty, with no music, no electronic clutter. He tried to recall his last afternoon in an English pub but the memories were a mish-mash, a garden, a wine glass in Hannah's hand, Liam on a swing. Twenty years, easily.

The decades melted, and here he was.

Flea Pointer came in, her tote bag a Penguin Classic design, *Brighton Rock*. Knowledge of what it contained dried his mouth.

"Mr. Bettany?"

"Tom," he said. "What are you drinking?"

"Maybe a mineral water?"

"You're asking?"

"I don't normally drink in the afternoon. And I already . . ."

"It's not a normal afternoon."

"Wine then. Red. Thank you."

When he returned from the bar, she'd taken her coat off and put the bag under the table.

He placed her drink in front of her, and sat.

Flea Pointer had a face that at first seemed flawed, with a slight imbalance that could easily have a man staring at her to work out precisely what was off-kilter, whether it was her mouth turning up at one side more than the other, or her eyes falling askew. Before long he'd have studied his way into a belief in her face's perfection. That was not how Bettany wanted this encounter to go. He continued his appraisal anyway, noting that she'd changed since the service, and now wore a dark-blue jumper that reached mid-thigh, and jeans tucked into brown boots. She'd tied her hair back, but a wisp fell across her forehead.

She was aware he was studying her, but trying not to show it. Concentrating on her wine glass instead, she adjusted its position on the beermat.

He said, "So you worked with Liam."

"That's right."

"I don't actually know what he did."

"Really? I mean—yes, sorry. I knew you weren't speaking."

She paused, but that wasn't a space he planned to fill.

"Vincent makes video games. *Shades?*"

She'd already told him this.

"It was really popular. A big seller."

"And Liam did this? Wrote computer games?"

"He was helping develop the vision."

He could sense quote marks around the phrase.

"And you?"

"I'm Vincent's PA. And kind of office manager. He's . . . not great with staff."

Bettany said, "How big is big?"

"Big?"

"As in big seller."

"Oh. Huge," Flea said. "Enormous. It made a ridiculous amount of money. Vincent went from being your standard issue geek, writing code in his bedroom, to one of the gaming world's heroes. There was even a movie."

"They made a film of a computer game?"

"You don't get out much, do you?" She touched his hand briefly. "I'm sorry, that was flippant."

"What made it such a hit?"

Flea Pointer sipped her wine. The time it had taken her to get round to this, Bettany had finished his Guinness.

"What was good was, it was totally unexpected. It looked like an arcade game, you know? The kind where you have an animated character doing the same thing over and over. Like collect all the bananas a monkey throws before you end up completely covered in bananas . . . This doesn't mean anything to you, does it?"

"Pretend it does."

"Okay then. As you know, there are two kinds of game."

She flashed him a look, saying this. He guessed she might be dangerous, in the right circumstances.

"There's the kind we've just been talking about and there's the adventure kind, the shoot-em-ups. Basically, in the shoot-em-ups, your character has a gun and you have to kill all the aliens or terrorists or whatever before they kill you."

"I grasped the concept with the name."

"Right. So at first glance *Shades* looked like one of the first kind, a low-spec affair. Except there was more to it. There was another game hidden underneath, and once you cracked how to get there, you were in a different place altogether. Suddenly . . ."

"You were in a shoot-em-up."

"The premise was that the world you started out in, the one where the characters just shop and do other boring tasks, was being controlled by this lizard race, and perhaps I should stop there? You're not looking convinced."

"I'm not much for computer games."

"No? Well. Enough people are to have made Vincent very rich. Like I say, he wrote *Shades* in his bedroom. He has staff now, and the company went public last year. *Shades 3*'s out in the autumn. That's going to make a lot of people happy."

"And make him even richer."

Flea said, "Not really."

Bettany raised an eyebrow.

"Nothing. It doesn't matter."

"How'd you end up working for him?"

"I answered an ad. Not everyone gets head-hunted."

Bettany wasn't sure what to make of that either.

She said, "You don't know, do you?"

"Don't know what?"

"It's a famous story. In the gaming world ... Liam didn't apply for a job with Vincent. Vincent went looking for Liam."

Bettany waited.

She said, "When I said *Shades* was a hidden game, I meant really. Hidden. There was no clue in the packaging or anywhere. It was up to someone to find it by accident. And that was Liam. Liam was the first to uncover the secret."

"And that impressed Vincent."

Flea began to speak, then changed her mind. She sipped wine. Her lips glistened red, until she ran her tongue round them.

"I guess ... I think Vincent always knew someone would crack *Shades*. And that when it happened, it would be big news among gamers. So once he found that the guy who cracked it was here in London, hiring him was too good a story to miss. And Vincent knows the value of a good story."

"But if Liam had been in Taiwan, he wouldn't have bothered."

"I doubt it. Mr. Bettany—"

"Tom."

"Tom, we're all so sorry about Liam. Vincent too. He'd have told you that himself if he'd known you were there."

Which sounded a polite lie.

"How close were you?" he asked.

"Me and Liam?"

He waited.

"We were friends. Not . . . We weren't dating or anything. But we'd hang out."

"You knew he smoked dope?"

To give her credit, she held his gaze. But instead of answering she took another sip of wine. At this rate, she'd be on her second by closing time.

At last she said, "Maybe."

"How does that work? Maybe you knew and maybe you didn't?"

"I meant . . ."

She trailed off.

"There's an idea," he said. "Tell me what you meant."

The door opened and men in football kit came in, smelling of sweat and exercise, filling the pub with noise. Bettany didn't take his eyes off Flea Pointer.

Who said, ". . . I only meant, look, I'm sorry, I know it's hard to hear this, but Liam was twenty-six. If he smoked a little dope now and then, it doesn't mean anything. He had a good job, and it's not like he was a stoner, you know? He just used it to relax."

"And how about you?"

"How about me what?"

"Did you get high with him? Was that one of the things you did when you 'hung out'?"

"Mr. Bettany—"

"It's just a question. Do I sound angry?"

He didn't sound angry.

"So a simple yes or no will do."

"Sometimes," she said.

Bettany didn't reply.

"Not often. Maybe three times?"

She made it a question, as if Bettany had been there, and counting.

"Okay," he said. "So this dope, where did it come from?"

"... Mr. Bettany?"

"Liam get hold of it himself, or did he smoke yours?"

"I'm not sure I want to answer any more questions."

"You probably didn't want to see Liam cremated either. Life's tough. You smoked his, didn't you?"

She said, "Usually."

"Usually?"

"Always. I've never ... I wouldn't know where to get hold of it."

This seemed to embarrass her. It was as if she were confessing to never buying her round.

"And where did Liam get it?"

An eruption of noise from the bar signalled a successful joke. Glasses rang and money was slapped on wood. A coin dropped into a slot and buttons were punched and the jukebox came to life, its opening notes meeting groans and more laughter. Through all of which Bettany's gaze remained steady.

Flea said, "Liam said he usually ... scored at a local club. I think he always went to the same guy, because it felt safer that way. But really, you know, it's not like it's ... It's barely even against the law any more. It's not like we're talking about, I don't know, coke even."

Yeah, because that stuff'll kill you, Bettany thought.

Perhaps the same notion struck Flea Pointer, because she coloured.

The music was getting louder, making the pub seem twice as full. What had been a quiet corner would soon become a crush. This wasn't a part of the city that saved itself for the weekend, if such parts existed any more.

Flea reached under the table.

"This ... Here. This is yours."

She pushed the bag across the table.

"I'm so sorry. About everything."

He nodded.

"I don't know whether you ... I mean, there's a garden of remembrance at the crematorium. Or maybe there's somewhere special ..."

He said, "Did he say which club?"

She didn't pretend not to get his meaning.

"No," she said. "He didn't say which club."

He nodded again, collected the tote bag, and left.

1.9

So now he was perfectly balanced, Liam's money in his pocket, Liam's ashes in his hand. Bettany carried the bag by its handles, scrunching them to reduce their length. When he'd hung it from his shoulder, its cargo banged his hip.

He had more than enough cash to get drunk. He was out of practice at London drinking, but it wouldn't be hard to pick up. It was dark, and the evening was swallowing landmarks. The city, like all cities, was offering anonymity.

Anonymity was what he'd need, in London.

So he walked the streets and checked what was on offer. It was early for clubs but pubs were available, and wine bars. Other places, he had no idea what they were. Literally. He passed a window through which white walls shone, art hung at well-lit intervals, and he'd have thought it a gallery if there hadn't been people unfolding menus and laying tables. Every twenty paces, the world changed. Now he was passing a bookie's and a boarded-up salesroom, now a string of takeaways, Bangladeshi, Japanese, Thai. A dentist's surgery next to a sex shop. Down a sidestreet brickwork was festooned with graffiti, pop-lettering so stylised he couldn't make out what it spelt. Beyond that a six-storey building shrouded in canvas, presumably for construction purposes, though the resulting blue cube resembled an artwork.

You might wonder if this was a functioning district, or just put on for show.

Among the exhibits, a man wandering the streets, his son's ashes in a bag.

Time was they must have walked hand in hand but that was so long ago it didn't feel like history, more like scenes from a film watched late one night, not paying proper attention. By the time Hannah grew ill, Bettany's relationship with Liam had fractured beyond repair. Afterwards, there was just the one argument. They had it many times but it was the same one, based on an equation Liam had discovered, tested, and found unanswerable. If Bettany had been a better husband, better father, better man, been around more, Hannah wouldn't have died.

That was how the young saw things. If that, then this. If this, then the next thing. Life, to the inexperienced, happened in straight lines.

Besides, he had been there. His job over, he'd been there for Hannah, for Liam, was making a proper family the way Hannah wanted. But by then, it wasn't just the three of them. It was four, the newcomer being the tumour in Hannah's brain.

You might find her behaviour ... erratic.

Always good to have advance warning.

What kind of erratic? he'd asked. As if there were an established procedure he could expect to unfold.

He was told paranoia was not uncommon.

As it turned out, advance warning was no help when Hannah ceased to be herself and became the voice of the tumour. Or was she simply venting long-suppressed feelings about his failures as husband, father, man? And how often had Liam overheard her outbursts, which would spring from nowhere? Over breakfast, calm as Sunday morning, she'd look up from her paper and ask how long he'd been fucking Meryl Streep. Or talk about the real family she hoped to be reunited with one day. She'd had names for them, a husband and two daughters. Her proper life.

Assailed by these thoughts, he needed another drink fast.

He chose a bar rather than a pub. Laminate flooring and a circular staircase in a corner leading down to toilets. Behind the bar, bowls of lemons and limes next to a wooden chopping board.

With a frosted bottle of Mexican beer Bettany sat with his back to a wall and watched the crowd develop. The bar was on a main road, and traffic shunted past in stop-start rhythm. Young people drifted by, the girls displaying more leg than the weather warranted, the boys wearing saggy-crotched jeans, their underwear showing. A fashion first practised by someone taking the mick, not that Bettany was an expert, or even welcome here. When he'd ordered a drink the girl had glanced across the room, as if checking with someone before serving him. Whoever the someone was must have been elsewhere.

He wondered if Liam had come here, whether it was the sort of place Liam had liked. He had no idea of his son's tastes. Late son. Whether he preferred beer, wine or spirits. Vodka and tequila seemed the current trends—had Liam swum with the tide, or followed his own inclinations? This gave Bettany something to think about while a young man approached. Black, smartly turned out, neat goatee so short it was near invisible. A nametag read TOBIAS.

"Enjoying your drink, sir?"

Bettany studied the bottle. It was kind of piss, to be honest. Maybe that showed on his face.

"So you'll be leaving after this one then."

"Is that a question?"

"We have a smart code, sir. I was round back when you arrived, or I'd have pointed that out."

"So I don't meet your standards."

"Nobody wants trouble."

Even for a mid-week evening that was taking a lot for granted, Bettany thought.

He said, "Mind if I ask you something?"

A raised eyebrow seemed to be acquiescence.

Bettany reached inside his coat, and the young man tensed. But when Bettany withdrew his hand, all it held was Liam's photo.

"Ever seen this man before?"

He'd nearly said *boy*. But the boy was long gone, even more impossibly distant than the man.

"You a cop?"

"Don't cops have a smart code too?"

Tobias glanced at the photo.

"He doesn't look familiar."

Bettany tucked it away.

"You work for the bar?"

"Can't you tell?"

"I meant, this actual bar. Or do you come through an agency?"

"I work for the bar."

"Only I thought that's how it worked. That door staff, whatever you call yourselves, were supplied by agencies."

"We get called lots of things. Some places use agencies, yes. But not us. Nearly finished?"

"Other places round here use them?"

"I'm sure some do. Looking for employment, sir?"

"Lately I've mostly worked with meat," Bettany said.

"That's perhaps as well. No offence, but we're encouraged to maintain high standards of personal hygiene."

"Got me there," Bettany said.

He drank half of what remained in his bottle and stood.

"Is it still true that it's bouncers push most of the drugs round the clubs?"

"I think you need to leave now."

"Ever heard of muskrat?"

"Now."

Bettany went.

1.10

The next bar had a bouncer in place, Asian, a barrel of a man in black tie who barely spared Bettany a glance. Further on was a pub, which was more inviting—had a blackboard boasting, with a hint of desperation, of the plasma screen on offer, and the match now kicking off—but Bettany kept walking.

He was heading away from Liam's flat. The streets were busier, people out to find a good time or leave a bad one behind, and the air was thickening with cigarettes and traffic and fast food. Smokers huddled round doorways, making stepping out of a modern pub like stepping into an old one.

Pasted to a bus stop window was a missing poster, a Chinese woman. She looked painfully young.

He stopped at the next bar, whose bouncer wore a T-shirt. When he showed him Liam's photo the bouncer stared. At Bettany, not the photo.

Bettany said, "Do you recognise him?"

"Nah."

"Have you looked?"

"Move on, yeah?"

Bettany put the photo away, but stayed where he was.

"You're blocking the pavement."

"I was looking to score some dope."

"You were *what*?"

"You heard."

The bouncer said, "Funny man. We do open mic on Saturdays. You'd need to tidy up, though."

Bettany moved on.

"And lose twenty years," came floating in his wake.

Something wild was tugging at him, something reckless. Maybe a little of Liam's connectivity, telling him *because of that, this.*

One thing happens, so the next thing follows.

Someone sold Liam muskrat, so Liam smoked it.

In a pub off the main drag he showed the bartender Liam's photo, and got another slow response. Asked whether there was a problem with drugs in the area, and got told nothing. Asked again, and got told to leave.

He left a full pint on the counter, unpaid for.

Bettany looped a circuit, looking for he didn't know what. He cut through a playground near an estate comprising a pair of '60s blocks. Dark oblongs limned in light were drawn curtains, and discs fixed at tangents to balcony railings were TV dishes. The playground was swings and a seesaw and plastic animals swaying tipsily on big springs. A five-a-side pitch carved out by ten feet of wire mesh occupied a corner. A red pinprick winked in the darkness at its far side. He didn't slow down but watched it glow and fade, and be passed along, and felt the air grow thick again.

On his second go-round, they emerged from the shadows. Three of them, kids, two boys and one he wasn't sure, but probably a boy. All mixed race. The tallest called from behind the mesh.

"What's in the bag?"

"Nothing you'd be interested in."

"How you know what I'm interested in? You know something about me?"

Bettany said, "You guys smoke weed at all?"

"That what's in the bag?"

"No. I'm looking to buy."

"You got money in the bag?"

"Ever heard of muskrat?"

The tall one laughed.

"We hear of muskrat? That's sick."

The one who might have been a girl made a gun out of finger and thumb, aimed it at Bettany's head. *Pkoo*.

"You a paedo, man? That why you hangin' round?"

Pkoo.

Bettany walked on, tote bag in hand.

Invisible, painless bullets struck him dead every step of the way.

He visited more pubs, asked more questions. Nobody was glad to see him. Even those who might have cared, who didn't take him for a cop but a parent tracking a runaway, wanted him gone.

"He looks old enough," said one woman, still in her teens. "He probably just wants his own life, you know?"

Some places he asked about drugs, whether they were a big problem round here. This wasn't popular either.

His first serious run-in came on neutral ground. He'd stopped to collect his bearings and decide which street to try next, knowing that whichever he took there'd be somewhere, a pub, a bar, a café, he could imagine Liam entering. A barber's window threw his reflection back as he stood there, and in this same window he saw them approaching, a matching pair. Tweedledum was barrel-chested, wore sleeveless leather, and the tattoos gracing his arms formed an intricate narrative that might repay study. Tweedledumber had opted for facial piercings. Both were stubble-haired and lightly goateed.

"You're bothering people."

It came scraping out of Tweedledumber's mouth as if some of those piercings had rusted on the inside.

Bettany didn't pretend innocence.

"Just asking a few questions."

"There's a Citizens Advice up the road," Tweedledum said. "You want answers, there you go. Anywhere else, mind your own business."

"Message received."

"I hope that's not a piss-take."

Bettany raised his free hand, palm open. "I'm not looking for trouble."

"Keep being a bother, it'll find you anyway."

For a moment longer they remained in formation, making it impossible for him to get by without squeezing between them. Then, as if operating on a frequency only they could hear, they moved aside, like an electric gate.

Bettany passed through.

Raging Angels. Neon Twist. Nightclubs had once striven for sophistication—Downtown Manhattan, The Mayfair, Tuxedo Junction. These days, implied threat seemed the norm.

Just short of eleven, he walked into a club while its guardians were occupied. Big front doors gave onto a red staircase with a wide mirror at the bottom, and another door guarded by a youth wearing a MADE IN BRIXTON tee. He did a double-take on seeing Bettany.

"Friend of Tommy's," Bettany said, dropping one of Liam's twenties on the table and sliding by.

It wasn't heaving, but there was a respectable crowd for a Tuesday in a recession. The bar was on a mezzanine with the dance floor below, visible through railings, and looking to Bettany like a wine cellar, stone walls and shallow alcoves. The music was mostly bass, and coloured spotlights looped and spun, overpowered every few beats by klieg lights drowning everything in thick white glare. He turned his back. What did he know? He must look like a bible illustration come to life. A girl shrank as he passed, making a *bleuch* face for her friends.

The floor round the bar was carpeted. Fibres clung to his boots.

Finding a gap he leaned on the metallic counter, earning another double-take, this from a barman with punched ears, polo mint-sized plastic disks allowing a clear view through his lobes. Instead of serving Bettany he turned and called a name. *Rowf? Roof? Ralph?* No way of telling.

Rowf or Roof or Ralph was more substantial in terms of years as much as girth. He and Bettany between them had more miles under their belt than the rest of the crowd combined.

What Ralph or Roof also had was a weary expression on a craggy face and a stubby index finger the size of a sardine tin. He crooked it to make Bettany lean forward, then said low and close, "On your bloody bike. Now."

Bettany showed him not Liam's photo, but another of Liam's twenties. "Quiet word?"

Ralph—probably—pursed his lips.

"Just some information."

A hand dropped onto his shoulder, and Bettany knew the door staff had caught up with themselves.

Ralph plucked the note from his hands.

"Time to go, Methuselah."

He hadn't been wrong about the bible illustration.

"I'll be outside," Bettany said, but Ralph was gone.

The door staff weren't rough with him, which he suspected was because they didn't want to get too close. It had been a while since he'd stood under a shower.

On the street they led him to a corner, one on each side.

"You're making a nuisance of yourself."

"Keep it up, and you'll attract the wrong attention."

"So do yourself a favour and go home."

It was like being the straight man in a musical. Maybe they'd break into a tap routine. When they didn't Bettany shrugged, and made as if taking their advice.

1.11

But he didn't. Instead he waited over the road in the doorway of a vintage clothing company, which had probably once been a secondhand shop. He gave it five minutes, then another five. At length Ralph emerged, lit a cigarette, and shared a laugh with the bouncers before setting off medium pace, a man on a break, no particular place to go.

On his side of the road Bettany held stride. Between them a hiccuping flow of traffic, mostly black cabs.

He let Ralph pick his own spot, which turned out to be a widening expanse where the road bled into a roundabout, from the centre of which an office block sprouted. On its side a huge advert, a Premier League name modelling a pair of briefs. Ralph leaned on a railing and lit another cigarette.

When Bettany reached him, he said, "You've got till I finish this."

Bettany showed him Liam's photo.

"Cop?"

"No."

"Private?"

"Do I look like a private detective?"

"Don't know," Ralph said. "Never met one."

He took the picture. Unlike most others, he studied rather than glanced at it.

"Maybe," he said. "I think so. Maybe."

He handed it back.

"Not a regular," he said. "But now and again."

"In a crowd?"

"That's how most people come. Unless they're just out to score."

"Score what?"

This earned him a slow look.

"What do you think? No one goes clubbing hoping to go home alone."

"What about drugs?"

"You are a cop."

Bettany said, "The boy. He's my son."

"Yeah, I figured. No offence, but if he was a pick-up, you'd have made more effort."

"He's dead."

Saying the words aloud was like hearing them the first time. Standing there, his boy's ashes in his hand, it felt as if he were just now getting the news.

"Sorry, man. Tough break."

Quickly said, but it sounded sincere.

Bettany said, "He was high. When he died."

"Damn."

"I'm looking for whoever sold him the drugs."

Again, saying it made it true.

A clique of women sallied past, perfume trailing in their wake.

Ralph ground his cigarette under a boot.

"You're kidding, right?"

Bettany waited.

"You're planning on going Bronson on the streets of N1? Two things wrong with this picture, man. You are nobody's idea of a vigilante. And you've pissed a lot of people off already, in case you hadn't noticed."

Bettany said, "You think that might have been in your club?"

Exasperation now. "What might?"

"Where he bought what he was on."

"Christ. Look, you've had your twenty quid's worth, okay? I'm sorry about your son, but seriously. Go home and mourn. You have got a home?"

"You want to meet him?"

"What now?"

Bettany held up the bag.

"My son."

Ralph stared. Then said, "You really are a whackjob, aren't you?"

"I hadn't seen him in a few years. But I figured we'd have time. I thought I'd run out of that before he did."

A sixteen-wheeler trundled by, navigating the roundabout the way dinosaurs must have waddled round waterholes.

Ralph said, "Look, I'm not saying nobody ever snorted a line in the toilets, but we're talking recreational. People get high to keep dancing. There's nobody sticking needles in themselves, nobody selling it to them. Not where I work. Wrong demographic."

"What about dope?"

"You'll need to be more specific."

"Cannabis. Weed. Marijuana. Whatever it's called now."

"He was smoking *weed*? For real?"

Bettany said nothing.

"Look, man, no offence. I mean, sorry for your loss, but he was smoking *weed*?"

"Muskrat, it's called."

"Yeah, that's seriously . . . That's mellow shit. You know? Look, sorry, but what happened, he fall under a bus or something?"

Bettany didn't answer.

"He did, didn't he?"

"He fell."

"Yeah. Look, I'm sorry. Really. But if he'd been drunk, would you be picking a fight with Smirnoff? It doesn't make sense, that's all I'm saying."

He turned to go, then turned back.

"Here. I don't need this."

This was the twenty-pound note Bettany had given him. He pressed it into Bettany's hand.

"Go home, yeah?"

He headed back to his job.

Bettany stood while traffic blasted round the junction, filing off in separate directions, the city, westward, further east. Way overhead an aeroplane silently circled. Eventually he stuffed the money into his pocket.

He left the main drag. He was not far from the playground where he'd encountered the kids smoking dope, which was not far from the pub where this odyssey had begun. A wave of exhaustion almost flattened him. He'd been awake a long time.

Carrying Liam's ashes had become central to his being. As if the bag's handles had fused with his fingers, the pair of them holding hands again across an unbridgeable gap.

Passing another bar he hesitated, unsure whether he'd tried

this one. Through its fuzzy-glassed window elongated shapes shimmered, and even on the pavement Bettany could feel music's dull thump, like a blunt-skulled creature repeatedly butting its head against a door. Not unlike his own evening's activity. This was enough of an insight to persuade him to walk on by.

A dog trotted past and disappeared up a lane. He followed it, thinking to cut off a corner, but the lane right-angled then dead-ended in a blank expanse of wall. Three wheelie bins stood sentry, each lid tilted by a bulging load of refuse. He turned. He wasn't alone. Blocking the way were a pair of large shapes, the streetlight behind them rendering their outlines harsh.

It wasn't a big surprise. The bouncers, Tweedledum and his shadow. He'd been warned off and it hadn't taken. They'd told him to go away, but here he was.

He said, "I was just going."

Neither replied.

"So no harm done."

Tweedledumber shifted his weight from one foot to the other.

"Okay then."

A car passed by out of sight, its throaty progress a reminder that he could have kept walking. Should have kept walking.

Tweedledum said, "Thought he'd been told."

"Definitely. He was told."

"We told him, didn't we?"

"We did."

"I distinctly remember that."

Bettany understood they were a comedy act, if only in their own minds. That this was the part they really enjoyed, or enjoyed nearly as much.

"But he's back."

"So he is."

"Bothering everybody."

"I get it," Bettany said. "I really do. I'll go now."

"Oh, now he's talking."

"Telling us he's off."

"Which is what he already told us."

"Except here he is."

A tapping noise had been going on for some moments. It came from the baseball bat in Tweedledum's right hand. He was gently bouncing it off the ground, testing its springiness.

Bettany said, "You're not seriously planning on using that."

"Seriously? We thought we'd already been serious. But apparently we weren't serious enough. Were we?"

"Not enough," Tweedledumber agreed.

"But what we find is, a little lovetap on the kneecaps, everything gets clearer. Says more than words ever can."

There was a rasping sound as Tweedledumber struck a match against the alley wall. When he applied it to the cigarette in his mouth, his face became an October pumpkin.

He dropped the match in the gutter.

Tweedledum hoisted the bat, slapped its thick end into his left hand.

"I've made a mistake," said Bettany.

"That you have, sunshine. That you have."

They stepped forward, and the punishment began.

PART TWO

∙ ∙ ∙

2.1

In the morning London exhaled, and its breath was foul. It swam
upwards from drains and gutters. It formed pockets of gas in
corners, and burst in noxious clouds from cars' rear ends.

By eight the first swell of workers had flooded the city and
the second was gathering force. The underground, arteries hard-
ening, was a wheezing queue of trains in which passengers,
squeezed into awkward shapes, counted down the stations of the
cross. Bad things could happen on the tube, though few entertained the possibility that disaster would happen to them. They
feared, instead, small acts of rudeness and aggression, their own
as well as others', because in the daily anonymous crush it was
easy for a grip on the ordinary decencies to loosen. The underground birthed a creature that might turn on itself. There was
little need of outside agency.

Among their number this morning, as usual, was a woman
whom even the kinder passengers would have difficulty not finding ugly. She was five foot tall and bottle-shaped, not classic Coke
but pale ale, straight up-and-down to the neck, with, today, iron-
grey hair whose colour matched the aspirin-sized growth that

bloomed on one side of her nose. But her eyes were piercingly bright, and she was expensively dressed—Caroline Charles, the discerning might have recognised, before wondering why someone wearing Caroline Charles chose to ride the tube at rush-hour. On closer inspection, they might have decided she resembled the more benevolent kind of witch, the type to dish out helpful potions when love let you down.

But few would spare the time to frame the thoughts. All were focused on being first off the train when it stopped. The woman seemed less anxious than most, allowing those around her to disembark before she did. On the stairs she kept an unhurried pace, not minding when less-controlled individuals rushed past, their disorganised limbs brushing against her. Once outside the commuters rediscovered their individual selves, and the temporary monster they'd assembled broke into parts and scattered. Her own course took her across the junction where traffic had argued itself to a standstill and onto a quieter road by the park, where a gracious terrace faced a row of full-grown sycamores, their branches leafless but no less soothing for that—*bare ruined choirs* her first thought on seeing them. *Where late the sweet birds sang.*

She ascended the steps to one of the grand buildings, and its door opened before she reached it.

"Good morning, Graham. All well?"

She slipped her gloves off as she spoke.

"Everything fine up topside, ma'am."

"All we can ask." Removing her scarf, she folded it over one arm as she crossed the hall with its wide staircase and the monumental Landseer on the wall. "You take care of things up here, and I'll do my best with everything else."

"Then we're all in safe hands," Graham said, as he did most mornings.

Dame Ingrid Tearney smiled, and stepped through the door to the left of the staircase.

Since 7/7 she'd used the underground at least once a day, always during rush hour, and made no secret of it. Every profile written about her, every interview she gave, the fact was tripped out. And she always gave the same reason, which, first time she delivered it, appeared in a round-up of that year's soundbites.

"My job is to keep our citizens safe. There's no risk they face that I won't gladly meet myself."

Do you think it's wise, she'd been asked, describing your average Londoner's journey to work as a risk?

I think it's wise that no one takes safety for granted, she'd said.

Despite the publicity she was never recognised, of this she was certain. She'd never been an agent—her route to head of the Intelligence Service had been largely via committee—but she had her smarts, and few illusions about herself. She sometimes drew a second glance, and knew full well why. But if she ever drew a third it would be someone realising who she was, and that never happened.

It helped, of course, that her hair alternated between the iron grey, a much curlier black and a really quite buttery blonde. Her wigs were expensive, age-appropriate, and functional. From the age of fifteen, Ingrid Tearney had been completely bald.

And now she was heading down again, the lift carrying her three floors below the street to the bi-monthly inter-departmental catch-up labelled W&N on everyone's calendar for Wants & Needs, but called by her Whines & Niggles. Not usually a meeting she'd chair, for the good reason that it made her want to murder her staff, but every other blue moon she'd turn up to demonstrate how hands-on she was, and spend two hours listening to departmental rivalries disguised as strategic planning. Why Comms needed extra space Intel should be made to surrender. Why Surveillance required a budget hike that could come out of Ops' surplus. Et cetera. They could type it all up in January and circulate it at intervals, the effect would be the same.

Which was what she found herself saying out loud to the assembled company—twelve department reps, a minute-taker and one extra—ninety minutes later.

"We have increasing demands placed on capped resources, yes. Explain why this always comes as a surprise? If you wanted free rein and unlimited funds, you should have gone into the City. Next time let's have less squabbling and more constructive thinking, shall we?" She removed her glasses, a sign that the meeting was over. "And let's not forget, when we drop the ball, lives are lost. There's no excuse for losing focus. Mr. Coe, would you stay behind?"

JK Coe was the extra.

After the others, seven men, six women, had trooped out of the meeting room, Dame Ingrid reached under the desk and disengaged the recording device. She then regarded Coe, a slight man in his early thirties, hairline receding already, wearing what she'd have to call a reserved expression.

"For all the backbiting, that was actually more muted than usual," she said. "Care to guess why?"

"Because I was here, Dame Ingrid?"

She waved away the title. "Every last one of them was watching what they said, for fear of hearing it quoted back at them in their annual appraisal."

JK Coe was from Psych Eval.

"Which means that if anyone wonders what you were doing here, that's the answer they'll come up with."

He said, "So that's not the actual reason you wanted me here."

"No. And I'd apologise for making you sit through that, but time spent working up a cover is never wasted."

Cover.

"This is an op?" he asked.

"Ops need approval from the Limelight Committee. I don't know where they get these names."

"They're selected randomly from—"

"This doesn't need approval because if it did it would be an op, and if it were an op it would require a budget ticket, and I've just spent an hour and a half repeating that this year's budget's stretched as far as it'll go. Does that answer your question?"

It wasn't an op.

Which was both a relief and a disappointment. JK Coe had never been involved in an operation. He was backroom, evaluating deskbound staff for their likely responses under extreme stress. Bio-attack stress. Terror event.

"No. Think of it more as a welfare assignment, one that nobody else need know about. Because if they did . . ."

"It would require a budget ticket."

"I'm glad we're on the same page."

Ingrid Tearney laid her palm flat on the buff-coloured folder in front of her.

"You know, the Service used to take pride in the fact that we looked after our own. Something else that's fallen prey to budget considerations. These days, once you're out the door you're history. But I've always had a soft spot for history."

When she paused, he assumed he was being invited to speak.

"How ancient a history are we talking?"

"Oh, relatively recent. Before your time, but you're one of our fresher talents, aren't you?"

Somewhat mesmerised by her gaze, he nodded.

Eleven months. Coe had been with the Service eleven months. A degree in psychiatry had derailed into banking, which had proved both lucrative and unsatisfying. The switch had been a good move.

That's what he thought so far.

Her eyes still on him, Tearney pushed the folder across the table.

"It doesn't leave the building. But you'll be more comfortable in the library. If anyone asks, you're reviewing this morning's minutes."

Bending back the cover, he took a quick glance at the folder's contents. It was stickered Priority John, the lowest of that year's five-tier security codes, and had x-s stamped in black on the top-sheet, meaning ex-service. A personnel file, one of thousands, relating to someone who was no longer part of the brotherhood, sisterhood, of agents. The photo showed a blond man with an army haircut and serious eyes.

THOMAS BETTANY, the caption read.

Dame Ingrid Tearney was standing so Coe stood too, tucked the folder under his arm, and left the meeting room with enough purpose in his step that anyone watching might imagine he knew precisely where the library was.

2.2

Psych Eval was based over the river. This was the first time Coe had entered the sacred precincts, as they called Regent's Park that end of town, which was why he'd been the only one at the meeting with a lanyard round his neck, VISITOR in red caps on a laminate. Nothing to say which department he was from. As he stepped back into the lift, having been told at the security desk where the library was, he wondered what made Tearney sure the others would have known who he was, rendering them suitably nervous—apparently—then answered his own question in the same serious tone the voice in his head adopted for work issues. They'd have known because she'd have told them. Sometimes things were that simple.

Even if unexpected.

Coe had colleagues who'd been with the Service ten times as long as him, and never had a phone call like his last night. *Dame Ingrid Tearney for JK Coe*, spoken as if she were her own PA, though it was the Dame herself on the line.

"I have a task for you."

A task. Like something Hercules might have been set.

"Be at the Park. Nine sharp."

The call had come after twelve, and he'd spent the rest of the night wondering if it was a prank, like that time in Uni when he'd received an anonymous note from a secret admirer, begging him to meet her in a nearby pub. Keeping the date was an act of folly which the bastards who'd set him up never allowed him to forget.

This morning, sitting through an interminable meeting, he might have wondered if this weren't some slightly more grown-up version of the same trick if not for the incontrovertible fact that at the head of the table, never so much as throwing a look his way, sat Dame Ingrid herself.

A Service legend, in her way. Not a bona fide legend like your Jackson Lambs—the plural uncalled for, because there was only one Jackson Lamb, thank God—but definitely a story in the making. Carving the Service into her own image, in spite of all those who queried the value of her initiatives, forever sucking up to Washington, spearheading charm offensives and doing wall-to-wall media. Taking the Intelligence Service "into the community." And, most sinful of all, not letting the fact that she was nobody's idea of photogenic—was, as one of those naysayers had put it, a crone in a designer cloak—ever hold her back.

Designer cloaks, he thought. JK Coe didn't know much about women's fashion, but Tearney had a reputation for dressing well. She could afford to, having private income, which she'd neither married nor been born into—was something of a whizz on the money markets. Maybe he should ask her for pointers, once he'd read the folder.

The library should have been all wooden shelves and high windows, in keeping with the Service's Oxbridge image, but was underground, with plain tables more suited to a canteen. Coe identified himself, found a corner, and settled down to read.

Thomas Bettany.

Bettany had been Ops, which was to say he'd seen undercover service, Northern Ireland at first, then in the capital itself. Martin Boyd had been his workname, and as Boyd he'd been a key figure in a syndicate run by the Brothers McGarry, a pair of charmers who'd supplied arms to a wide variety of customers, from armed robbers to at least one budding terrorist group. It had been one of the longest ops the Service had run on home soil, and when it wrapped it claimed fifty-two scalps, including some MoD suits who'd been involved in diverting decommissioned materiel into the McGarrys' hands. This brought an end to Bettany's Ops career. After a stint with the Dogs, the Service's internal police, he'd taken a pay-off and relocated to Lyme Regis with his wife and son, presumably to set about rebuilding a family life his work had left in tatters. This hadn't lasted. Painfully soon afterwards his wife, Hannah, was diagnosed with an inoperable brain tumour expensive care had done nothing to render otherwise. She'd died within the year.

Once widowed Bettany had drifted abroad, surviving on labouring jobs. Detail was sketchy, but there'd been a covert status-check within the past year. He had been in Marseilles then, working in an abattoir, and a contacts list included just one name, a colleague named Majeed Ansari. A faint pencil mark under this surname suggested that someone had lingered there a moment.

Coe didn't know what to make of any of this. Had Bettany been sucked into the netherworld that often snared X-Ss, turned mercenary or worse? Dame Ingrid had called it welfare. Maybe Bettany was sick, or off the rails. Some huge percentage of home-less people, he didn't have figures to hand, were ex-military. Perhaps he'd fallen prey to that syndrome. Did Tearney expect Coe to come up with a rehab plan? And why him, only eleven months into the job? Not knowing what he was supposed to be doing he did it again, to be sure, then one more time. Thomas Bettany. By the time he left the library, JK Coe could have taken him as a specialist subject.

There was the hub, Regent's Park's nerve centre, where the Second Desks oversaw the current emergency (and there was always a current emergency), and then there was Upstairs. Upstairs was where Dame Ingrid sat. Head of Service was informally known as First Desk, and with First Desk came a view.

So Coe, on his first-ever visit to the sacred precincts, had a view of the park opposite, a cool green breathing space—he felt like he'd climbed ten rungs of the ladder since midnight.

Few of his colleagues would have seen this coming.

Because he hadn't lit bonfires, JK Coe. Wasn't one of those others kept an eye on, in the expectation of glory to come. He knew that. But he also knew his strengths, which, if unexciting, were valuable enough. He was conscientious. He was thorough. He was careful. When you gave him a task, he'd do it in the time allotted—or at the very least, remain behind until it was done. He nodded now at Dame Ingrid's greeting, and settled in the chair she'd indicated, the folder on his lap.

Many men, pushed to describe themselves, unconsciously add an inch or two, here or there. Coe's tendency was to subtract. He felt shorter than his 5 foot 9, and while he recognised this was an esteem issue, nevertheless often found himself shrinking to fit. He'd even cut his forenames down to size—Jason, Kevin. Neither could be taken seriously. It was an unaccustomed twitch, then, that he felt in First Desk's office. Like a novice dragged from the chorus and thrust into the terrifying spotlight, he was discovering he kind of liked it. If this was a test, he was hoping to pass.

The chair was dependable, high-backed, upholstered. The laminate round his neck hung comfortably against his shirt.

Dame Ingrid said, "You've read the file."

He nodded.

"So tell me what you make of him." She threaded her fingers together, as if about to show him the church, the steeple. "In one word."

"Violent," said Coe.

She raised an eyebrow.

He said, "He survived years among the worst this city has to offer—gun runners, real gangsters—and he did that by becoming one of them. So convincing, there was no telling him apart."

She said, "He wouldn't have lived through it otherwise."

"I know. I'm not making a moral judgment. He's a highly trained operative, and violent was part of his job description. But from the redacted passages, it's pretty clear he overstepped a line somewhere. In the interests of . . . authenticity."

"You think he hurt someone."

"At least. Yes."

Dame Ingrid refrained from nodding thoughtfully or gazing at him in an assessing sort of way. She simply waited.

"Afterwards, his record as a Dog—I mean—"

"I know what they're called."

"He developed a reputation for being strong-arm."

That part of the file had been sufficiently redacted for Coe to feel secure about drawing this conclusion.

"Not that I'm suggesting he went way out of line. And his resignation seems genuine. I mean, he wasn't eased out, far as I can tell."

It hadn't escaped him that Dame Ingrid had been First Desk when Bettany left the Service. If there'd been anything more to the story, she'd know it.

He said, "When his wife died, there was some kind of bust-up with his son."

"What makes you say that?"

"Because Bettany's reaction to her death was to walk away. If they'd got on, they'd have mourned together, helped each other through. Instead, Bettany dropped everything and seems to have spent the last four years doing menial jobs in some pretty rough parts of mainland Europe."

A part of Coe, listening to himself, was dropping his jaw. First thing you learned in Psych Eval was to hedge your bets. That seemed less useful at Regent's Park.

Or maybe just in Dame Ingrid's presence.

Who said, "So why the labouring?"

"There weren't details—"

"You don't need them. He was highly trained, not uneducated, and he's just spent four years emptying Spanish bins and lugging French meat. What was that about?"

She didn't have the air of one who would appreciate waffle.

JK thought about his answer for a moment. Tried not to think about anything else, such as why he'd been plucked from his niche for some off-the-cuff theorising about a one-time spook he'd not heard of till an hour ago. Tearney didn't seem to mind waiting. It was something she was good at.

He said, "I doubt it was his wife's death sent him into a spiral. It was probably the bust-up with his son."

"Why?"

"His wife was sick a long time. He'd have had time to prepare, emotionally."

Dame Ingrid said, "Lots of parents fall out with their off-spring. Fathers with sons. They don't all emigrate. Fall into a 'spiral.'"

"They don't all have Bettany's background. A lot of ex-soldiers become homeless. When the structure they've based their lives on is removed, everything else falls apart. Bettany wasn't a soldier, but he was of the same mindset."

Coe was in a landing pattern now.

"He'd spent the best part of a decade undercover, pretending to be someone else. In short order he'd quit his job and become a widower, wasn't a husband any more. Now he wasn't a father either, or so it must have seemed. It's not difficult to see why he went the way he did."

Now the atmosphere shifted. He could tell that new information was on the way, something not included in the folder.

Dame Ingrid said, "His son died last week."

"Ah," said Coe.

"He fell from a window."

". . . A high one?"

"In a manner of speaking. He was smoking cannabis at the time."

Dame Ingrid brought her chin to rest on her fingers.

"Now," she said. "What would you expect a man like Bettany to do under those circumstances?"

It felt to JK Coe like this was the point of the exercise.

"Well," he said. "Liam's death makes their estrangement permanent. However it must have felt before, there was always the possibility there'd be . . . reconciliation. He'd feel robbed of that."

"Robbed," said Tearney.

"Yes. And he's a man with a certain skill set. If he feels he's been robbed, he'll do something about it."

"Something?"

"He'll kill them," Coe said. "He'll go after whoever he decides is responsible, and he'll kill them."

2.3

Getting ready for work, dressed but still a mess, Flea Pointer had a meltdown. A small one, but. She was removing all trace of a minimal breakfast, a glass of fruit juice, a cup of coffee, and was standing by the sink when she was overwhelmed by pointlessness. Not just of rinsing the cup and glass but of everything. Her friend was dead and she was trying to pretend he wasn't, because how else could you interpret this attempt at normality? Getting up, getting dressed, getting breakfast, was all part of making ordinary life carry on, of tarmacking over Liam's ineradicable absence, as if his death were a pothole which might in time be fixed.

Worst of all, there were no tears. There was just sadness, and a weary knowledge that even though she had these feelings today, there would come another morning when she would not, and the tarmacking-over would have begun in earnest.

The lobby buzzer rang.

It was a rule of hers not to speak when the buzzer went—the world was full of stalkers—so she lifted the receiver and waited.

"Ms. Pointer?"

It took her a moment.

"... Mr. Bettany?"

She pressed the button to let him into the building.

It didn't take him long to reach her floor, but long enough for her to wonder if she'd done the right thing. She was already running late. What did he want now?

But when she opened the door, all that was replaced by a more immediate response.

"What happened to you?"

"What do you mean?"

"Your face—your head ..."

"It's just a cut."

"*Just?*"

Bettany said, "Never seen a man with a haircut before?"

He'd lost the beard too. It made him ten years younger.

"Can I come in?"

They were standing in her doorway.

"Of course. Yes. I mean ..."

She stepped back, and Bettany entered her flat.

He looked fresher too, in new clothes, which with a pang she recognised. The collarless white shirt, the black V-neck, they'd been Liam's.

"Is everything all right?" she asked.

Bettany paused, looking round her sitting room, making swift inventory. Then he turned to her.

"Liam didn't fall," he said.

"I ..."

The word tailed away. This could turn out worse than she'd feared.

He said, "Can I smell coffee?"

"Just instant," she said mechanically.

"Mind if I ..."

Flea shook her head and he followed her into the kitchen, a nook off the sitting room. She flipped the switch on the kettle, found coffee, and shook granules into a cup. Questions about milk and sugar seemed too normal. She'd pour it black, and deal with complaints as and when.

He looked more like he ought to look now, she decided, not entirely sure what she meant. Blonder, certainly. Unbearded, his jawline was pale. He looked like he'd been through some stuff, but hadn't been battered into submission by it.

Handing him his coffee, she said, "What do you mean?"

"Exactly what I said."

"But that makes no sense. Of course he fell. That's how he died."

She was thinking, he never saw the body. Had he persuaded himself Liam was still alive? That some gruesome misidentification had occurred? It would be a good way of making everything right again.

But would involve ignoring reality.

He sipped the coffee, not seeming to mind it black, or very hot, and said, "He hit the road. That's how he died. But it wasn't a fall."

And now she could see where he was coming from.

He said, "He was getting high, right? Like he'd done with you those times you talked about."

"Only twice. Maybe three—"

"However many. What did he do, roll up on the balcony?"

"No," Flea said, then paused, remembering. "He'd roll up inside, a pair, which was usually enough. And then he, we, he'd go outside and light up there. He was kind of finicky about getting smoke in the room."

"What did he light up with?"

"A lighter. He was always losing them."

"Well, he lost the one he used that night too. Because it wasn't on the balcony, and it wasn't in his pocket. The policeman gave me his effects. No lighter, no matches."

She waited for more, but that seemed to be it.

He read this in her face.

"Doesn't seem like much, does it? But it's enough. He had no lighter, no matches. Nowhere in the flat. He could have lit up from the electric ring on his stove, but not without leaving traces, and there aren't any. And he hardly went back and cleaned up afterwards."

"Did you look on the balcony?"

"I looked on the balcony."

"Maybe he dropped it."

"In which case it would have been on the street below. And the police would have collected it. That's what they do. They collect evidence."

"Maybe he used a match."

"Just the one?"

"Yes. And it blew away."

"One match. Not a safety match, but a single red-top he could have struck off the wall."

"Yes."

"How likely is that?"

"Odd things happen."

"All the time. But this wouldn't just be an odd thing. It would be an odd thing happening moments before Liam died. Which is beyond odd. Which is suspicious."

Saying all this, Bettany remained calm. Those blue eyes, striking enough when he was unkempt and straggle-haired, looked ready to drill holes through walls, but he wasn't manic or excited.

He's found a place to stand, she thought. He's not going to be talked out of this. He's found a place to stand.

Bettany put his cup down.

He said, "He was smoking a joint without having the means to light it. That means someone else was there."

"It doesn't mean he didn't fall."

"Maybe not. But someone was there when he did. So why haven't they come forward?"

"Maybe they're scared."

"Scared? Because they were stoned at the time?"

"Yes."

"What's that amount to, a slap on the wrist? You said it yourself. It's barely even against the law."

"Still. He died. They must feel responsible."

Those blue eyes were fixed on her.

"Don't you think?"

She could hear her own voice faltering.

He said, "Was it you, Flea?"

"No."

He didn't repeat himself, didn't ask if she was sure. But he kept looking at her for a full seven seconds before nodding.

"Okay."

Flea found herself wanting to sit. Wondered if he was aware she was trembling.

"So," she said. "What are you going to do?"

His gaze shifted to nowhere in particular, an unfocused moment of thought. But he was back almost immediately.

"I need to know who it was. Which means I need to know more about Liam's life. The people he hung out with. His job."

"Speaking of which, I'm late. For work, I mean."

"That's okay," he said. "I'm coming with you."

The alley fight hadn't lasted long. The bouncers had been big and confident, but were used to this being enough and had come at him swinging like windmills. Bettany, in contrast, had been schooled to be precise and waste no effort. Only connect. The training stayed with you.

Afterwards, because they'd planned to break his kneecaps, he broke theirs. Then he'd wiped the baseball bat and dropped it by their feet.

Seven years out of circulation, but some things stayed in the blood. Walking back to Liam's, he'd felt alive. He didn't like to think it was the violence that had set him buzzing, but face facts. It hadn't been the beers.

At Liam's he'd searched the place the way he'd been taught. Bad didn't equal clever. The same hiding places, envelopes taped to the underside of drawers, baggies in the cistern, the key sandwiched by a magnet to the back of a radiator, cropped up over and over. Liam hadn't gone for any of these, though Bettany found his dope-stash without effort. But no lighter, no matches . . .

Confirmation acted on him like a drug. He'd barely managed

to pull his boots off before collapsing on the bed and dropping
into a dreamless state from which he awoke feeling fresher than
in years, though only six hours older.

When he flexed his fingers he felt the action at his knuckles.
They were grazed but just slightly. Months spent hefting meat
hadn't softened them up. Besides, he'd mostly used his feet.

After a long shower, he'd checked his finances. His stock had
risen by the precise amount he'd found in the bouncers' wallets,
so he was now holding three hundred and seventy pounds, plus
euros. There was more money, of course. Liam had a bank account,
savings, maybe insurance, all of which would have to be dealt with,
but not now. As for Liam himself, his ashes were on the kitchen
table. He'd have to make a decision about that too, but first things
first.

Liam's phone was in the sitting room. Bettany plugged it into
a charger then headed out to Flea Pointer's, whose address he'd
found pinned to the noticeboard in Liam's kitchen.

On the way, he'd passed the same barber's he'd seen last night,
open early for the office trade, and had thought, *High time.*

And now they were walking towards the Angel, en route to Lunchbox, which was what Vincent Driscoll's games company was
called.

"It's not far. A bus ride."

"It's a while since I've been on a London bus."

She said, "I don't suppose the experience has changed much."

Little had. There'd been a sharp rise in the number of women
reading bondage porn in public, but other than that, London had
stayed London.

The bus stop had an LED display. Their bus was seven minutes away.

"I'm going to be really late. I'm usually there first, by miles."

She was also going to be turning up with a dead colleague's father. Bettany didn't think her being late was going to bother anyone long.

The pavement was narrow, and the queue for the bus snaked down it. People walking past had to step onto the road.

Flea said, "He said some things about you. Liam did."

"I expect so."

She seemed ready to continue, but he gave her a hard look, and she refrained.

They'd been silent for a while by the time the bus arrived.

Flea led them upstairs. The bus moved slowly, negotiating what felt like endless roadworks. Rows of shops gave way to a railed-off patch of greenery, a church, a library. Ten minutes into the journey some kind of crunch point was reached, and most passengers departed.

She nudged him. "Move up."

To the front seat, she meant.

He complied, and now they had a view of the road ahead. Fewer roadworks, but plenty of traffic lights. Bettany had forgotten that getting round London resembled descriptions of warfare. Long stretches of boredom interspersed with moments of panic.

That, too, summed up much of his own career.

She said, "I didn't mean to upset you. I just thought . . . You didn't talk for years. Maybe you should know some of the things he thought about."

She was young enough to imagine words like *closure* had meaning.

He said, "You didn't upset me."

"You didn't want me to go on."

"Not right there, no."

"We're alone now."

They weren't. There were three others on the top deck, the nearest only three seats behind them. But it was clear Flea would think him pedantic if he pointed this out.

He said, "Liam needed someone to blame when his mother died. I was the obvious candidate."

"How did you know what—"

"He didn't exactly keep it a secret."

"No. No. But what I was going to say, Liam knew it wasn't really your fault, that he was just lashing out. Every time he talked about it, he got nearer to admitting it."

The bus passed another church, and they were briefly level with stained glass.

She said, "It was as if he was having an argument with himself, and becoming less convinced he was right."

The man three seats behind them stood and headed down the stairs, pressing the bell as he went.

"Liam said other things too."

She waited for him to ask, but Bettany wasn't rising.

"He said you used to be a spy."

"How long's this bus ride?"

"Our stop's next."

"Good," he said.

He'd formed no mental picture of Lunchbox's premises, but even so Bettany was mildly surprised when Flea led them onto the towpath towards what might have been a restaurant. The ground-floor was green-tinted glass with a logo of a child's lunchbox, plastic catch unsnapped, something unseen glowing within.

The towpath was stony, uneven. Twenty yards ahead a bridge spanned the canal, its arch a mossy curve.

Approaching the door Flea said, "Everyone's busy, you know. With *Shades 3*. I mean, everyone's sympathetic, we all loved Liam, but . . ."

"But life goes on."

"And it's not like you're police. We've already talked to the police."

"If you didn't want me to come, you should have said so back at the flat."

"I didn't think you'd take no for an answer."

"You got that right. Will Driscoll be here?"

"I expect so. You're not going to . . ."

She didn't seem sure what she was asking.

"Tender plant, is he?"

"He's a little sensitive."

Bettany hadn't had much practice lately at being around sensitive people.

He looked down at the canal's oily surface, its miserable rainbows.

"There was a man at the crematorium," he said. "Part of a group. They had flasks."

"I saw them."

"I don't think they knew Liam. I think they were there for the entertainment. The way some people hang out at weddings."

"Maybe. I guess."

"I'm wondering what else I might have missed," he said.

Flea said. "You didn't answer my question. You're not going to upset Vincent, are you?"

"I expect he'll survive," Bettany said, and stood aside as Flea opened the door.

2.5

Boo Berryman said, "**Who's** that?" then, "From which publication?" then, "Concerning what, exactly?"

Then, "He's not available now, but I'll be sure to pass that on."

He hung up and said, "A journalist. One of the gamer mags. Asking about Liam."

Vincent Driscoll, upright on the sofa in a manner that suggested it was stuffed with bricks, shook his head.

Boo said, "Monthly publication. By the time they print the news pages, they might as well label them history."

He'd been with Vincent six years, driver and general dogsbody. Before that he'd been a fitness instructor, but that came to an end when he landed badly from a climbing fall, cushioning the beginner whose fault it was. Who'd been grateful and mildly bruised. Boo still limped in damp weather.

But a bum knee didn't mean he couldn't take care of himself.

The car keys lived on a hook by the kitchen door. He let them slide onto his index finger like a set of knuckledusters.

"Ready to go, boss?"

Vincent nodded.

■   ■   ■

In the back seat, Vincent stared unseeingly out at boring streets, unremarkable events. Everything reminded him of everything else, because everything was all the same. He toyed with that thought for a moment, but it didn't lead anywhere.

The back of Boo's head was a bowling ball onto which some joker had pasted strands of human hair.

"What kind of name is Boo?" he'd asked, back when he'd interviewed Boo for the job. He couldn't remember the answer.

That had been about eighteen months after *Shades* went big, and Vincent had been the subject of newspaper profiles. The proper press, not just gamer mags. Ridiculous sums of money had been mentioned, most of them off target, but it turned out that made no difference. People who were uptight enough about other people's money to write ugly letters tended not to make fine distinctions. Add a zero, take one off, it was still an outrage. How could anyone get so rich off a game? Someone ought to teach him a lesson. Someone likely would.

Vincent had taken notice, taken advice, and found himself Boo Berryman.

Six years later he could count on one hand the days that had passed without Boo's presence. On the other hand, whole weeks could pass without Vincent laying eyes on anybody else. Which, it turned out, was eccentric. Rumours grew about his remoteness, his aloofness, his "high-functioning autism." But that was okay. People could say what they liked, provided they did it somewhere else, and didn't bother him with the details.

They did sometimes, of course. That was what Boo Berryman was for.

Who pulled up outside Lunchbox now, the street side.

Vincent got out while Boo went to park. He looked up at the building, which was three storeys high here, four round back, where the ground dropped to the towpath. Someone was watching from the upper window. Flea Pointer, but who was with her?

For one juddery moment he thought it was Liam Bettany.

The moment passed, and whoever it was stepped away from the window.

Vincent pushed the door, and entered his building.

2.6

Bettany's first impression was that Vincent Driscoll didn't look like a multi-millionaire. He looked like someone a multi-millionaire had picked from a crowd and dressed in expensive clothes.

When he said, "I'm sorry about your son," it sounded to Bettany like he was reading off an autocue.

Which fitted the surroundings. Lunchbox was immaculate. Bettany's experience of software-based, youth-oriented work spaces, absent anything in the way of heavy tools, was limited, but this felt familiar because he'd seen it in a dozen films. A big room, open-plan but with screens here and there, shiny metal furniture, abstract paintings on the walls, abstract chairs for sitting on, and a laptop on every surface. Vending machines were ranged along one wall, soft drinks and snacks, and someone was collecting a Coke without having fed the machine any coins.

A basketball net was fixed in a corner, and a soft orange ball lay on the floor beneath.

A whole bunch of people had read a whole bunch of magazines before kitting this place out.

Though Flea had worried they'd be late, they were still first to arrive. She'd made coffee, then showed him round—the open-plan downstairs area where Liam had worked with his immediate colleagues, the ground floor and the upstairs offices arranged around an atrium. It seemed a lot of building for a small company.

Flea said something about creative space, sounding like she was quoting someone.

"Why is nobody here yet?"

"It's not a nine-to-five gig. People work the hours that suit them."

It was nearly ten before they started to turn up.

If anyone recognised Bettany from yesterday's service, they didn't show it. If they minded his questions they hid that well too.

"We're all really sorry about Liam."

"We liked him."

"Yeah, we'd hang out. Fridays, we all hit the local."

"And sometimes a club afterwards."

"Not to dance, specially. Just for the laughs."

But when Bettany asked about Liam's friends outside work, he drew a blank.

"Don't remember any names."

"He must have had some, but . . ."

"I think there was a Dave. Was there a Dave? Or was that his brother?"

Bettany said, "He didn't have a brother."

And the pub, the clubs, the after-work life, had all happened in the same tight circles.

"Never went to his flat."

"Only ever saw him in a crowd."

Bettany said, "What about drugs?"

"Drugs?"

"He was high when he fell," Bettany said. "You must know that."

"The police were asking about weed," someone admitted.

"First I'd heard about it."

"We all like a drink, but . . ."

With their open faces, their guileless youth, they were definitely lying. But probably only about the weed.

Already he was having trouble keeping names straight. Names like Kyle and Haydn, Eirlys and Luka. All round Liam's age, though there was an older woman, a marketing rep. She touched his elbow, told him she couldn't imagine how it must feel, not having children herself, never having married.

After he'd gleaned as much as he was likely to without dropping the friendly pretence, he let Flea lead him upstairs, where the windows were untinted, and the view was of rooftops across the canal. What had once been factories were now flats, though retained the outward appearance of industry. But an industry tamed, its corners waxed and polished.

She said, "I think they were starting to wonder. You know, where grieving parenthood ends and interrogation begins."

"Trust me. When I cross that line, they'll know about it."

She led him into her office, which adjoined Vincent Driscoll's. A lot of one wall was window. Down below, Driscoll was emerging from a car. When it left he stood looking up, as if he sensed that Bettany, or someone like him, was watching.

For a moment, Bettany thought he was going to turn and walk away. Instead he'd pushed through the door and entered the building.

More impressions. Mostly of someone very clean, very neat, who probably spent ninety minutes getting dressed. But that might be as much to put off stepping into the real world as to impress anyone he met there.

His fair hair bordered on translucent. His skin too was papery, thin, as though Bettany could poke a finger right through him if the urge demanded.

Which it might.

"Can you spare a few minutes?" Bettany said.

This was clearly disconcerting.

"I don't usually see anyone without an appointment."

Bettany waited.

Flea Pointer said, "Mr. Driscoll's got quite a busy morning . . ."

There was a simple trick, one Bettany learned in his stint as a Dog. It was a matter of looking like you not only weren't going anywhere but were incapable of forming the intention. Like forests might rise and mountains fall before you'd move a foot.

Flea, about to speak again, changed her mind.

Driscoll made the mistake of glancing towards his office. Nearest place of safety. Bettany latched onto it as if it came inscribed RSVP.

"In there's fine."

Driscoll said to Flea, "When Boo—when Mr. Berryman arrives, could you send him up?"

"Of course."

Driscoll's office, if Bettany had been asked to guess, would be devoid of anything personal—just the usual chair, desk, desk hardware—and he was largely right, though hadn't banked on the big and vibrantly coloured poster boosting a movie called *Shades*. That aside, it was a room that looked easy to leave in a hurry.

Without waiting to be asked, he planted himself in the visitor's chair.

"Smart building."

"Thank you."

"All this from writing games?"

"It turns out you only need to write one," Driscoll said.

"The basketball hoop," said Bettany.

Driscoll waited.

"You get that from a film? Or read about it in some effective management handbook? How to encourage 'creative thinking'?"

Driscoll said, "I think it was Ms. Pointer suggested the basketball hoop."

"Everyone being free and easy. Let the ideas come swimming out."

"Something like that."

"Does it help?"

"If it helps my employees, that's fine. Personally, I don't . . . Why all these questions, Mr. Bettany?"

"I'm trying to get a handle on my son's life. Exactly how free and easy does it get round here?"

"I don't know what you mean."

"The kids smoke dope on the premises?"

"Of course not. That would be a sackable offence. And nobody wants to lose their job, not one where they're paid for doing what they'd do for fun. What do you do, Mr. Bettany? I don't think you said."

"Lately, I've worked with meat."

". . . I've no idea what that means."

"How well did you know my son?"

"How well . . . ?"

"Not a complicated question."

"No. It's just that, well, I didn't. Not really."

"But he worked for you."

"Obviously."

"Because he was the one first cracked your game."

Bettany gestured at the poster on the wall.

"That not give him special status?"

"It made him . . . a good hire."

"A good hire."

"There was interest. Publicity. Chatter on the web. Things you need in this business."

Which sounded to Bettany like something he'd learned by rote.

"So Liam himself was, what? Neither here nor there?"

"He was a good hire."

"Which anyone in his position would have been."

A slight nod allowed the truth of that.

"Did you ever visit his flat?"

"Mr. Bettany. He worked for me, that's all."

He made a fluttery gesture with his hands.

"My team are all good people. I'm sure they are. But . . ."

"But you're not a people person. Are you gay?"

"You think your son was my boyfriend?"

"I don't know. Was he?"

"He was my employee. I didn't know he was gay."

"I didn't say he was."

"You're obviously trying to trick me into some kind of admission, I have no idea what. I'm sorry about Liam, really I am. But I'd like you to leave now."

A slight disturbance told Bettany someone was in the doorway. It would be Driscoll's driver. Flea had called him some stupid name. Boo?

"How come your new game won't make you richer?"

"That's . . . I'm not sure what you're talking about."

But he was. Bettany could see it in his eyes.

Behind him, Boo Berryman coughed.

"I'll see you out," he told Bettany.

2.7

Berryman walked Bettany downstairs, where the kids were at their desks, glued to screens, calling to each other in what might have been code.

The woman who'd touched his elbow half-waved as they headed for the door, a movement she turned into a rearrangement of her hair when Bettany ignored her.

Outside Berryman said, "Finished now?"

"Finished?"

"Coming into Mr. Driscoll's workplace, upsetting his staff. Asking stupid questions."

Bettany guessed he'd been overheard asking Driscoll if he was gay.

"Making a nuisance of yourself."

He said, "Nobody seemed upset."

"They were being polite. On account of the situation."

"But you're not."

"I'm sorry about your boy. But I have my own responsibilities."

"Sure."

"Chief among them making sure nobody disturbs Mr. Driscoll."

Berryman spoke with assurance. He was usefully built, and the way he stood suggested he knew how to handle himself. Slightly favoured his right leg, though.

He was probably making his own assessment of Bettany.

Who said, "My boy wasn't alone when he fell."

"I didn't hear that."

"No, it didn't get much coverage. On account of whoever it was made themselves scarce."

Berryman didn't answer. But he tilted his head to an angle, as if he'd moved on from gauging Bettany's weight and was now wondering what kind of bullshit he was peddling.

Bettany said, "Until I find out who that was, I'll be carrying on doing what you just said. Making a nuisance of myself?"

"That was it."

"Good. A nuisance, then. Count on it."

"Mr. Driscoll had nothing to do with your son's death."

"Then Mr. Driscoll has nothing to worry about."

Unlikely to find a better line to leave on, he left.

Back at Liam's he opened a tin at random, heated its contents and ate them with a spoon. Afterwards he sat by the window. A cat was prowling its territory, coolly observed by a pigeon on the opposite roof. Ordinary small happenings. Liam must have witnessed a hundred such scenes, non-scenes, at this window, events which weren't eventful but just the inevitable consequence of time passing. Bettany withdrew but left the window open. Fresh air gratefully occupied the flat.

He was starting to feel he knew this room. The sofa looked less like someone else's furniture, more a personal invitation. He lay on it, feet hanging over the arm. This, too. How many times had Liam lain like this?

Bettany breathed in the odour of his son.

When he opened his eyes again, time had passed. He'd spent some of it thinking about Vincent Driscoll. An uptight individual, uncomfortable with strangers, but lots of people were. That whole business of hiring Liam for being the first to crack *Shades* might be on the level, and Flea's comment about the new game not making Driscoll richer, that might mean a tax fiddle, a charity wheeze, anything. Not Bettany's concern. Having a minder might be because that's what rich people did. But he was an odd duck.

As for the kids, whose jobs involved playing games, or talking about playing games, or working out new ways of playing games, they'd not been holding back anything important. In the Service, as a Dog, Bettany had interviewed professionals, people who'd been trained to lie and had a flair for it. He'd learned how to excavate falsehoods, scrape away the truths to find the treacheries beneath.

All of which had been long ago, and a mild conversation in the workplace didn't build up the pressure those interrogations had generated. But if there'd been anything to find, he'd have sensed it. Enough to know there was someone he'd need another crack at, somewhere less public. And there'd been nothing. Only Driscoll tripped his wires, and that might just have been personality.

Tripped his wires . . . A phrase from days gone by.

He checked Liam's phone, found it fully charged, and scrolled through the contact list. Flea, of course. Kyle and Haydn. Eirlys and Luka. And others, forty or more, some first names only, some with reminders attached ("dentist," "bank"). No way of knowing whether first-name-only indicated a degree of intimacy rendering description otiose, or acquaintance so casual Liam didn't know their surnames.

Well, there was one way of finding out. Reclining on the increasingly familiar sofa, he began the tedious process of calling them all.

Afterwards he lay dry-mouthed, Liam's phone on his chest. Most of those he'd spoken to had known of Liam's death, and of those who hadn't, one or two didn't have a sure grasp of who he was. And of those who recognised Liam's name but hadn't known he was dead, none seemed sure how to respond. It was as if they were being polled on a news item not relevant to their situation.

All of which confirmed Bettany's suspicion that his son had had no one truly close, Flea Pointer perhaps excepted. There were other avenues, of course, and might be a whole crew of buddies somewhere, boys he hung with, girls he slept with, but if so they'd made little impact on his surroundings. Work life aside, Liam seemed to have been a solitary.

He turned the phone off and went into the kitchen, where he poured, then drank, a glass of water. Wiping his mouth afterwards, he was struck by the strangeness of an only slightly stubbled chin. But that too would grow familiar. Everything did, in the end.

A hand on his chin . . . He experienced a sudden memory, as real as if he were thrown back in time, of his infant son, a few months old, reaching out and grasping him there. Then it ended.

There weren't many such memories. Much of Liam's childhood had taken place in Bettany's absence, while Bettany himself had been Martin Boyd, acquiring the habits and thought processes of a made-up man. Family life had been a series of snapshots, interrupting the movie. Brief, furtive visits, more like a passing criminal than a father. It wouldn't be hard to draw a connecting line between that and the life Liam had been leading, apparently successful, but lacking solid relationships. A case of the apple and the tree. Undercover, after all, was what Bettany did when his own life failed him. Undercover meant dropping from sight, leading somebody else's life in a succession of foreign cities. It meant leaving everything behind.

When Martin Boyd had been put to rest, and the Brothers McGarry were behind walls, Bettany had thought it possible to continue in the Service. He'd joined the Dogs, but it had been a failure. Something had boiled inside him, kept rising up the back of his throat. Short fuse, Psych Eval said. All those years of being someone else, he hardly knew how to be Tom Bettany any more. And London had become enemy territory, the chances of encountering someone who'd known him as Boyd a constant tremor in the background. Before long he'd taken a severance payment and moved the three of them to Dorset, a coastal town, a new life.

Bettany poured more water. He didn't often think about his past, but that too was the undercover mentality. The person you used to be was sealed off, boxed tight, locked shut, and you walked away. But nobody really walked.

Oddly, it was his stint in the Dogs he'd had trouble shaking off, once they were settled by the sea. Bad things happened in the noughties, and in the wake of attacks in New York, London, Madrid, Mumbai, policing the Service acquired a broader remit, the investigation and interrogation of undesirables. It had been a bad time to be undesirable. While the public records defined the Service's decade as one long cock-up, a lot of successes never made the papers because they left nothing in their wake. Men disappeared, women too, and those who'd known them were left under no illusions about their own fate if they kicked up fuss. Records were sealed. Names erased. The subjects never saw daylight again. Packed into aeroplanes, shuttled into godforsaken skies, they'd never stand trial or hear a human voice. Next time they opened their eyes, they'd see everything their future held.

Operation Waterproof. That was the name of the protocol.

Bettany had never seen these prisons, most of them in former Soviet states, which had no shortage of facilities and accepted all major credit cards. But he'd heard stories. They had no windows, no exercise yards, no visiting rights, no phone privileges. You didn't have to worry about being raped or knifed in the showers because there were no showers. There were cells, seven foot by five, with a door and a bucket. Once a week the bucket was removed, emptied, put back. The food never varied. For entertainment, you had the clothes you stood up in. After a while, even your memories would taste of stone.

On bad nights he dreamed of such places. It was every undercover agent's hell. A place where there was no hiding from yourself.

It had been a policy used in the worst of times, and he supposed it was used still.

Not his world any more.

It was early but dark already, and Bettany had plenty of sleep owing. On the sofa still, he collected on the debt.

His dreams were small, and tightly enclosed.

But he slept a long time, and didn't wake until his phone rang.

2.8

A **pair of police** horses clop-clopped past the following morning, their riders' heads on a level with JK Coe's, who sat on the steps of the National Gallery watching crowds throng Trafalgar Square. He waved a vague salute and the nearest cop, a blonde with her hair tied to match her mount's tail, nodded severely. Thinks I'm a civilian, thought Coe.

Even cold, damp, 11 A.M., the square was awash, rival groups of tourists kitted like football fans, sporting red cagoules or yellow sweatshirts. Their team leaders had umbrellas or sticks with bright pennants to raise whenever movement was called for or a head-count necessary, but until they were summoned the flocks swarmed at will, painting the air with their chatter.

"Meet him somewhere public," Tearney had said.

"Of course."

"And don't let him walk all over you. We're doing him a favour."

A regal sniff.

"I don't expect gratitude, but I do expect him to observe the decencies."

This, his second encounter with Dame Ingrid, had taken place earlier that morning. Instead of the office, the view, the mahogany furniture, he'd been instructed to wait near her tube exit, carrying an almond croissant in a Carluccio's bag. For identification? Surely she'd remember what he looked like? He hadn't dared ask.

The rest of yesterday he'd done legwork, or what passed for legwork in the age of Google. Interesting fact number one, a couple of bouncers had been scraped from an alley floor in N1 Tuesday night, kneecaps remodelled. "Slipped while moving a wheelie bin." But it wasn't far from where Liam Bettany had lived, and bang in the heartland of where you might go if you were looking for a score.

Interesting fact number two . . . Actually, fact one was as far as he'd got. The rest was static, the white noise you heard when you were looking for something but didn't know what it was. Coe wanted a bone to drop at Tearney's feet. Show her his quality. But bouncers aside, all he really knew was that Bettany was active, had spoken to a policeman, and was staying in his dead son's flat.

Tearney had emerged from the tube station a pulse behind a commuter surge.

"Walk with me," she said.

The morning traffic did what morning traffic did. Rain threatened, but kept changing its mind.

Dame Ingrid said, "What news of our friend?"

This was a test. If Tearney wanted to know what Bettany had been up to, she'd have had a three-inch thick dossier waiting on her desk. 10:03:02 P.M., Subject blew his nose. 10:03:04 P.M., Subject returned handkerchief to left trouser pocket.

He said, "He's doing what I said he would. Well, he'd already started doing it by then."

"Elaborate."

Coe told her about the bouncers.

"So he's looking for the drug connection."

"... Yes."

Tearney halted by the pedestrian lights. She was wearing a different outfit this morning. Coe himself changed his shirt more or less daily, his trousers twice a week, his jacket seasonally, but First Desk had to make an effort. Her raincoat was black, belted and reached to her knees, and Coe had no hope in hell of identifying it by label, but it looked expensive. Beneath it she wore a pale suit and neat black boots with a red buckle. That her hair today was a tight crown of black curls, Coe knew enough not to comment on. On her raincoat's collar a seam had pulled loose. He'd have pointed this out, but valued his prospects.

She said, "That didn't sound convinced."

The lights changed, and the green man beckoned. They crossed the road in step.

Coe said, "He didn't kill them."

"You're unhappy about that?"

"It strikes me as strange."

"Explain."

"Maybe they sold Bettany's son his dope, and maybe they didn't. I don't see that it matters either way. They were probably selling *somebody* dope, and that's all Bettany needed. This was never a job for Hercule Poirot. He went looking for pushers and he found a pair. So given who he is, what he can do, I don't see what kept him from killing them."

They weren't far from Regent's Park. Tearney wasn't leading them that way, though. Whatever this meeting's about, thought Coe, it'll be over before she heads for her desk.

Now she said, "Perhaps you're doing him an injustice. He

might be more targeted than you suggest. More focused. Less inclined to settle for a token victim."

"If he wants to find the actual dealer who sold Liam the actual dope he was smoking, he's going to have to dig around in his son's life."

Tearney said, "That does present a slight problem."

And Coe sensed they were arriving at the point.

The horses were past him now, leaving JK Coe with a view of their fine hindquarters. Animals built for dumping from a great height. Not for being dumped on.

A bus backfired and a clatter of pigeons took flight. Coe followed their progress into the grey mid-air, where they wheeled figure eights before settling back on the square and resuming their mindless milling.

And just like that he wasn't alone any more. Tom Bettany sat next to him, calmly watching pigeons and tourists, as if he'd been occupying that same spot for half an hour.

Coe said, "I don't need to ask who you are."

"I don't expect you do."

But then, he'd seen Bettany's Service photo. Bettany had put on a few miles, but fundamentally he looked the same.

His eyes were unnaturally bright, though. Coe wondered if he were on anything, and immediately answered himself, *No*. He was high on the task in hand, that was all. The same energy pulsing through him as in that alley, when he took apart the bouncers.

The thought unnerved him, bringing to mind Dame Ingrid's instruction. *Meet him somewhere public.*

He noticed Bettany's crooked smile.

"What?"

"You're thinking I'd better behave. Given how public we are.

All the good little tourists, mobiles at the ready. We're already on a hundred holiday movies."

"I've no reason for thinking you're a threat."

Bettany looked at him, still smiling. "Seriously?"

"To me, I mean. I'm here to do you a favour."

The ex-spook raised an eyebrow.

"This I've got to hear."

2.9

This is what Tearney had told Coe earlier.

"Bettany's son worked for a person of interest."

Person of interest ran the whole rainbow, from potential asset to suspected terrorist.

Coe said, "He's on a watch list?"

"No. But he's been vetted for a gong. Services to British software industry, or something. I don't recall the details."

The details, surmised Coe, were packed tightly in her head, and could be unfurled at a moment's notice, like ticker tape, or a till receipt.

"In addition to which he's being actively wooed by both HMG and the Loyal Opposition. Vincent Driscoll might not have much in the way of politics, but he's very much a British success story."

So nobody wants Bettany sticking his oar in, Coe thought.

"Of course," Tearney said, "there's no earthly reason why Thomas Bettany should want to make life difficult for Driscoll. But he's a loose cannon. And if, as you say, he's decided his son's death warrants investigation, and he starts poking around Liam's life, well, he's going to make himself unpopular."

"I'm not sure that'll worry him."

Tearney gave him a look.

"I hope you're not finding this amusing."

"No."

"Good. Because what I'd like you to do, dear boy, is have a word with him."

Was there ever a more transparent ploy than *dear boy*? And yet he couldn't say it didn't work. Here he was, walking the pavement with the head of the Service, and she was coming over all grandmotherly.

It made him want to genuflect.

"Meet him somewhere public."

"What if he doesn't—"

"Oh, he will. Once a Dog, always a Dog. He'll respond to a tug on the leash."

"And what do I tell him?"

"That Vincent Driscoll's out of bounds. Might as well have a Do Not Disturb notice round his neck."

She came to a sudden halt, and Coe marched a pace onward before noticing. He stopped and looked back.

"But be subtle about it."

He nodded thoughtfully, as if mentally working out the sly way he'd go about planting this idea in Thomas Bettany's head without Bettany being aware of it.

Dame Ingrid reached into her bag, and Coe was cast back decades, waiting dutifully while his nan dug about for a small treat, a coin or bar of chocolate.

What she came up with instead was an envelope. She handed it to him.

"And in return for being a good boy, Bettany gets what he wants. No need for him to wear out shoe leather turning over every stone in N1. Liam Bettany was smoking muskrat when he died. It's a new strain, which, luckily for us, means a restricted point of retail. The gentleman whose name's in that envelope imports all the muskrat smoked in Greater London."

Coe felt the envelope gain weight as he caught her drift.

He said, "Just so we're clear . . ."

"Yes?"

"Bettany gets a white card on dealing with this guy?"

Dame Ingrid said, "Oh, I think we can allow him a little latitude. And unless he's forgotten everything we taught him, he's not going to be caught afterwards, is he?"

A little latitude, thought Coe, adding it to his bank of euphemisms.

"But if he gets a bee in his bonnet about Driscoll, that's a different story. He'll be dealt with."

"Should I tell him that too?"

"Oh, he'll grasp the idea. And I'm sure you'll keep me abreast of things."

He was being dismissed. But there was one more thing he wondered about.

"Why has Bettany been taken off the Zombie List?"

"Error? You know what records are like," said Tearney. "But that suits us fine. We don't need him setting off unnecessary alarm bells. He'll want to keep a low profile too, come to think of it. London's not exactly packed with his old friends."

And now she was holding her hand out expectantly.

For a moment, Coe thought she wanted the envelope back. Evidence. Destroy after reading. But that wasn't what she was after.

She said, "My pastry?"

Dumbly, he handed the bag over.

"Thank you."

Tucking it under her arm, she headed off towards her kingdom, a short stout woman few would give a second glance.

Despite the chill, Coe found he was sweating.

Compared to Dame Ingrid, he thought, Bettany should be a breeze.

And now here he was, following instructions. Meet him in a public place. Let him know who's in charge.

The public place bit had been straightforward enough. Convincing Bettany he was in charge might prove more challenging.

Testing the waters, he said, "I'm from the Park."

"Uh-huh."

"Ingrid Tearney."

"She still First Desk?"

"They'll have to chisel it from her grip."

"And you're her messenger boy."

So much for being in charge.

Bettany said, "Thing is, I haven't actually done anything, other than ask a few questions. Unless you think messing up a couple of bouncers calls for a slap on the wrist. But even if you did, know who I think wouldn't?"

Coe was already regretting using her name.

"I can't see it crossing Ingrid Tearney's desk, let alone her mind. So what's going on?"

Coe said, "We're sorry about your boy."

"Is that a confession?"

He was already surrendering. "No no no no no. All I meant was, you have our commiserations."

"Why? It's seven years since I left the Service."

"Still . . ."

From here they had a view of the Mall, where something was happening now, a black limousine appearing, flanked by police motorbikes. As one, the tourists turned to check it out. It was like watching wind sweep through a field of corn. Mobiles whirred and cameras popped.

Despite himself, Coe wondered who it was, and decided it was probably a prince. One of the older, useless ones nobody liked.

When he turned back, Bettany was studying him.

"You're not Ops," he said. "An agent wouldn't have sat here, and wouldn't have been ogling a cop while waiting for a hostile."

"You're not a—"

"An agent treats any unknown as a potential hostile. So you're virgin, or as good as. And you're what, thirty-five? Four?"

Coe didn't dignify that.

"So you're a desk jockey, but if you were a Park desk jockey that would make you Strategy or Policy or whatever they're calling it now, and they don't let those guys make appointments with strange men in public places. That's the last thing they let them do."

Bettany paused. The car with its prince or whoever had vanished. The crowds had reconfigured, or maybe were different crowds. The pigeons were almost certainly the same ones, though.

"So if you're not Park you're from over the river, which is where they keep the pointy heads, the ones who do the touchy-feely stuff, like work out who's stressed, and how much time off they should get. Stop me if I'm hurting your feelings."

"Don't be ridiculous."

"So why do I get a phone call from an over-the-river virgin, summoning me to a heads-up? That's what you called it, right? A heads-up."

Of the possible outcomes Coe had pondered, being laughed at hadn't figured.

"Finished?" he asked.

Bettany wasn't.

"Know how many times I encountered Dame Ingrid, back in the day?"

He made a circle with finger and thumb.

"This isn't because she has fond memories of you."

"Yes, I got that. It's because she's worried I'll step on the wrong toes. And I can guess whose. Not like I've been mixing with more than one millionaire lately."

Coe tried not to react. He sat, hands on knees, his gaze directed at a group of Japanese holidaymakers photographing each other against the backdrop of the fourth plinth.

"So Vincent Driscoll's an untouchable. That's the message you're delivering."

"Vincent Driscoll's uninvolved. That's all."

"And you don't trust me to work that out for myself?"

"We thought it might be simpler if we helped you cut to the chase."

Bettany shook his head.

"You're going to help," he said. "Why doesn't that fill me with confidence?"

"Why, what's your plan? You're going to leave spatter marks everywhere anyone's selling dope?"

"I'm sensing aggression."

"If Dame Ingrid wants to help, it's because she doesn't want an ex-agent running rampage through London. Not even the bad parts. You plan to leave the country when you're finished, right?"

"What's it to you?"

"It will be all round tidier." Coe reached inside his coat. Bettany's hand caught him by the elbow.

Coe said, "Please. Be my guest."

Bettany's hand eased into his pocket, and relieved him of the envelope he'd been about to produce.

"You want me to précis?"

"Is it in code?"

"No."

"Then I expect I'll manage."

He stood to go. As he did so the police officers clop-clopped by once more, the blonde one regarding them with that impassive curiosity police cultivate. Bettany responded in kind and once they'd passed turned to Coe again.

"What's your name?"

Coe told him.

Bettany nodded, and left.

Alone on the steps Coe inhaled deeply, finding the air colder, as if he'd been sucking on a mint. *He needs to know Vincent Driscoll's out of bounds. Has a Do Not Disturb notice round his neck.*

But Coe wasn't sure whether he'd warned Bettany off or tied a firework to his tail.

PART THREE

3.1

Leaving the National, Bettany headed west, into the maze of Soho's skinnier streets. Twice he changed direction abruptly, causing no giveaway ripple. This didn't mean he wasn't under surveillance—cameras brooded over every last alley of the capital—but the lack of hard bodies rendered it unlikely. If he warranted serious coverage, they'd not have sent a featherweight like Coe.

Satisfied, he slipped out of the byways, and on a bus heading along High Holborn made some calls.

Bad Sam Chapman had been Head Dog until leaving the Service under a cloud, a cloud the shape of the huge sum of money that went walkabout on his watch. These days he worked for an agency, tracing runaways and bad debts. The Chapman Bettany remembered must have had to make serious adjustments, among them getting used to being easier to find.

He didn't sound different. A tightly wrapped bundle of irritation back in the day, civilian life hadn't cheered him up any.

"I heard you'd dropped off the map," he said, without sounding surprised Bettany had dropped back onto it.

"Miss me?"

"No."

"I need a favour."

"And I need a pension and a hair transplant."

"You always did," Bettany said. "Griping about it now won't help."

Chapman hung up.

Bettany waited a minute then rang again.

"I don't do favours," Chapman said, "and I don't do memory lane."

"Liam died."

Chapman said, "Shit."

Then, after a moment's shared silence, said, "What kind of favour?"

A bull terrier was going apeshit near the railings, racing around under trees in which two, no, three crows were flapping about and cawing. The crows were messing with its head, taking it in turns to dip close before flapping upwards again and settling in branches while the dog tore circles, one tree to the next, barking like its heart would burst.

Bettany had taken up station here, half a mile or so from Liam's flat. He found it easier to think in the open air. Distractions like the dog stirred up thoughts as busily as it scattered leaves and dirt.

The crows laughing. The dog near exploding with rage.

Bettany's phone rang.

"Marten Saar," Chapman said.

This was the name in Coe's envelope.

Chapman said, "There's a new strain of weed on the market, they call it—"

"Muskrat."

"And Saar has a lock on it. Give it four months, six tops, it'll be everywhere, but right now, buy any round these parts, you're putting money in his pocket."

"And nobody's shut him down?"

"Shocking, isn't it? You think he's paying someone off?"

"I was thinking more of the competition."

A crow screamed from the safety of a branch.

"He's Estonian. Showed up here in the '90s, probably because of turf wars. Been a mid-level player since '06, but this muskrat business has him on the upswing. Rumour says he's in talks with the Russian mafia."

"'Talks.'"

"Yeah. They wear suits and everything. Second banana's also from the old country, one Oskar Kask. The whisper is Kask's the brains, but he moonlights nicely as a thug. He's the reason the competition have held off. Nobody wants to cross Kask."

"Record?"

"Kask was picked up after a Hackney wannabe called Baker died of a hole in the head last year. Released without charge. But . . ."

His voice trailed off.

"But he did it," Bettany finished.

"Well obviously he did it, but the CPS passed. Either he's got a hell of a lawyer or . . ."

Bettany filled in the blanks. Or Kask, or Saar, or both, had Plod connections.

"Where are you now?" Bad Sam asked.

Bettany's reply adjusted his actual location by a mile.

"You can probably see Saar's house from there. I say house. Tower block. Lives up on the top floor like a king in his castle. And," Bad Sam Chapman said, "you'll have to get past his pitbulls."

"Actual? Or are you being picturesque?"

"Picturesque."

The real-life dog was approaching a canine aneurysm.

"What about that other address?"

Sam read it out, while Bettany listened. Notes were for amateurs. Clues waiting to happen.

Finishing, Chapman said, "I wasn't kidding about Kask. He's vicious."

"Noted."

"Be careful."

"On that subject . . ."

"No."

"I didn't say anything."

"You were going to ask if I can get you a gun. The answer's no."

"It was worth a try."

"You've been away a while. Things aren't like they used to be. The stakes are higher. Those Russians I mentioned? Word is, they're the Cousins' Circle."

The Cousins' Circle was high-calibre all right. The Amazon of the drug-trafficking world.

"So what are you planning?"

"Bit of light shopping."

"Seriously."

"Seriously, I'm not planning anything," Bettany said. "Not until I've verified some stuff."

Putting his phone away, he left the park.

The dog's mad barking rattled in his ears for blocks.

In a cycling-supplies shop off Old Street he found a long-sleeved high-vis tabard with silver shoulder-banding. At the till he was asked if he'd thought about upgrading his machine, and truthfully responded that he hadn't. In a stationer's he bought a clipboard, an A–Z and some parcel tape, then cleaned the next-door super-market out of thick black plastic binliners.

His phone rang again as he was leaving.

Flea Pointer.

"I can't believe you asked if he was gay."

He negotiated his way around a pair of young mothers, double-pramming the pavement.

"He told you that?"

"I was next door."

A clock above a jeweller's told Bettany it was after two.

"Are you finished now?"

"Finished what?"

"Asking questions."

"Not yet," he said.

"Only I was a bit worried. The way Boo walked you out yesterday?"

Boo. Bettany still couldn't get his head round that.

"Vincent's just a softie. But Boo used to be some kind of fighter? Olympic standard, someone said. And he's very loyal to Vincent."

"You like him, don't you?" he asked.

"Boo?"

"Driscoll."

"Yes. No. I mean yes, I like him, but not like that . . ."

"Is he gay?"

"I don't know."

"Was Liam?"

"No. I don't know. What difference would it make?"

"None."

She fell silent.

"My turn to ask," he said. "Are you finished now?"

"You can be quite hateful, you know."

She ended the call.

Next stop was a hardware store, where he bought a small toolkit and a length of clothesline.

The days of the A–Z were numbered now people had Google maps on their phones, but phones left digital footprints while a paperback stayed dumb. Studying it, Bettany felt London's geography returning to him. Unless it had never gone away but just been overlaid by other cities, whose shapes were fading now, the way architecture dims at twilight.

He'd been aimed and pointed, which was nothing new. For years that's what he'd been, what he'd done. It was since he'd been cut loose that everything fell apart.

Some rules still held good, though.

When given a free steer, verify. That was one.

Also, *When pushed, push back.*

Tucking the A–Z away, he headed for the tube.

3.2

There was no sense having a car in London. This was received wisdom, undermined only by the number of cars there were here, there, everywhere in London. JK Coe had identified the unspoken codicil, that there was no sense having a car in London unless you had a parking space. Then there was every sense having a car in London, even if you had to leave it in your parking space, to stop anyone else parking there.

That wasn't going to happen to JK Coe. His parking space was underneath his building, with his flat number posted to the wall above it, and the white lines marking its dimensions touched up every year. It had added more than a few K to the price of the flat but that was fine, because sensible or not, there were never going to be fewer cars in London, and when it came to selling up, he'd at least double the more-than-few K he'd shelled out, back when he was earning big bucks in banking. This thought, or something like it, went through his mind pretty much every time he parked his car. He'd got it down to a moment of mental shorthand. *Car/space*, he'd think. And the ghost of a smile would tickle his lips, as much a part of the process as locking the doors.

There was a lift and an emergency staircase. He always intended to take the stairs, and always didn't.

Today, on his way up to the fifth, his mind was on the evening ahead. He liked being at home in the city, glass of wine in hand, looking out at the lights of London, tracing in their winkings and blinkings thousands of stories he'd never know. It made him feel like a poet, if not the kind who ever wrote a poem.

But when the lift reached his floor, he stepped out into darkness. This was odd because the maintenance charge was steep, and any lapse in the facilities leapt on sharply by the residents' committee, but Coe didn't dwell on it because the dark of the hallway was instantly matched by an equal darkness inside his head. There was no warning. One moment he was in the dark, and the next in a deeper dark. The opportunity to comment was denied him.

Time passed. When he opened his eyes, he couldn't be sure where he was. The immediate sensations were localised—pain, cold and fear. The pain was a dull throbbing behind his right ear, from the blow that had rendered him unconscious. The cold was because he was naked. And the fear . . .

The fear was because he was bound to a chair, his wrists lashed to its arms, his feet to its legs. A cloth plugged his mouth. Everything in sight—the floor, walls, curtains, the strange shapes that were presumably furniture—had been draped in black plastic. Binbags, whole rolls of them, taped together and plastered across everything. There was only one reason anybody would do such a thing. Coe felt the fear plummet through his body, invading his stomach, his bowels. It fogged his vision, and as a further realisation stuck him—that this was his own sitting room, rendered dungeon-like by black plastic sheeting—it grew wings, as if he were carrying inside him a giant bat, which was even now clawing its way free.

Then Tom Bettany appeared, stepping through the doorway that led from Coe's kitchen. He too was naked, apart from a pair of latex gloves. In his hands, Coe's own electric carving knife.

JK Coe fainted as his bowels let slip.

More time passed. Probably only moments. His own stink had filled the room, and Bettany had plugged in the carving knife, making a small hole in the black plastic through which to thread the flex. He measured its length, then placed the knife on the floor. Coe spoke, or tried to. *Mmmpff mmmpff mmmp*. Bettany passed behind him and Coe felt the chair being shunted nearer the knife, to within its reach. *Mmmpff*. A liquid slap was his own shit hitting plastic.

That was what the binbags were for. To leave no marks, to make no mess.

Bettany had made himself a sterile environment.

Mmmpff!

The chair settled back on the floor.

Coe pulled against the clothesline, which wouldn't give. He hurled himself sideways instead, and the chair toppled, and he was down, head banging on the floor. Immediately he was hauled back upright, the chair made straight again.

Bettany's head was close to his.

"Don't."

Then Bettany stepped away and retrieved the carving knife, sliding the button on the handle with his thumb. How many times had Coe done that? Hardly any, truth be told. Maybe a dozen. Mostly the knife lived in its drawer, an unnecessary gadget bought because buying unnecessary gadgets made the western world go round. Its buzz was familiar, nevertheless. Like an electric toothbrush, but with more edge.

And he was naked. Coe hadn't been this close to a naked man, he didn't know in how long. School gym? Never in his own flat, never at close quarters. Bettany was naked because things were going to get messy, and Coe had an uninvited image of Bettany's clothes, neatly folded, on Coe's own bed. Somewhere he could easily get dressed again, and walk away spotless. He swallowed, or tried to, but his mouth was dry and full of cloth.

Mmmpff.

Bettany turned the knife off and laid it on the floor. Nude, he looked stronger than when clothed. Coe did not want to be noticing this. Didn't want to see the muscles moving easily underneath Bettany's skin, his penis and testicles dangling unashamedly between his legs. Coe didn't want to be near a naked man, full stop. A naked man with an electric knife, he wanted to be far away from.

He tensed against his bonds once more. There was no give, no slack.

No chance.

Bettany disappeared into the kitchen but was back within moments, carrying the carver's spare blades. Coe squeezed his eyes shut, but couldn't help hearing the clatter as Bettany laid them on the floor. Somewhere in the kitchen, on a shelf, was a booklet explaining which blade suited which task. There were illustrations of joints of beef. How to cut against the bone. How to carve through knotty passages.

There was a rustling, and Coe could feel the other man's heat as he knelt and bent in close again.

"Do you know what a professional would do?" Bettany's voice was calm. "A professional would hurt you straight off the bat. Badly. To establish the perimeter. To let you know who he was, and what you were."

It was growing harder to keep his eyes closed. He wanted to open them, let morning light burst in, *that was the worst dream ever*. But was terrified, too, that that wouldn't happen. That he'd still be here.

"Call me an amateur, but I'm not going to do that, Coe. Which is as much of a break as you're going to get. And if that turns out to be a mistake, all I can say is, I intend to clean up afterwards. Understand? Nod your head."

Coe nodded his head.

"Okay. I'm going to ask questions. You're going to answer them. Any hesitation, any hint you're not telling the truth, all of it, and you know what happens."

There was a brief whine as Bettany snapped the electric knife on and off.

"I'll start with your toes, but don't think that means you get ten shots. I'm not a precision carver, Coe."

He whimpered again.

"But I have worked with meat."

Bettany pulled the cloth from Coe's mouth.

3.3

"**T**earney really sent you?"

"Yes."

"Why you?"

"Because . . ."

His mind blanked.

The blade whirred.

"Because I'm not Park."

"Say more."

"It's not an op. Not official. Off the books."

"Just the two of you."

". . . Yes."

"Why the hesitation?"

"Nothing. No reason. Just the two of us, yes."

Bettany stood behind him, heat coming off his body.

"And she told you to give me Marten Saar."

"Yes."

"Why?"

"Because he's the source, he imports it. Muskrat. Which your boy was smoking . . ."

"And that's the reason."

"The only reason."

"Because you thought that's what I'm after. Payback."

"I knew you'd gone looking . . ."

"For Saar?"

"For anyone. For a source in the trade. Someone to . . ."

"Kill."

Coe didn't want to hear the word. Didn't want it loose in his flat.

The stink, his own, already hung in the air.

Forever after—if there was a forever after—he'd always know how he'd reacted to danger, and the knowledge would always diminish him.

"Was it a set-up?"

"What?"

"Were you trying to put me in play?"

Bettany was prowling now. Coe could hear his feet on the cold black plastic.

"We were trying to help you. Give you what you wanted."

"And you decided I wanted Saar."

"I told you—"

"Or maybe you wanted Saar out of the picture."

"I'd never heard of him before this morning."

"But Tearney had. Maybe she thinks I'm her toy soldier all of a sudden."

And now he was back, all but resting his head on Coe's shoulder.

"Is that why you gave me his name? Because Tearney wants rid of him?"

"I . . ."

"That's not an answer."

"I don't know."

Bettany withdrew. Those slinky footfalls again. Eyes tight shut, Coe willed himself into any other evening but this.

Home from work.

Glass of wine.

Lights of London.

Not tied to a chair with a naked man threatening to mutilate him.

But this was where he was, and this was what was happening. And it was Thomas Bettany doing it, a man whose file he'd studied. Could he have predicted Bettany would do this?

Stupid question. He hadn't.

A buzz from the electric knife, and he yelped.

"You're drifting."

"Sorry! I'm sorry . . ."

The buzz disappeared. But its electric pulse still wormed into his ear.

"You said you don't know. So maybe Tearney's playing me."

"All I know is what she told me."

"Tell me again."

"That nobody wants you running rampage through London. Taking revenge wherever you find it."

"Really?"

"Yes. She said if you took out Saar, got rid of him, that would be enough. You'd go away, back where you came from, and that would be that. Game over."

Mentally, he was making calculations. At what point would anyone notice he was in trouble? There were emergency protocols, panic numbers, a six-minute response. But you had to ring the panic number first.

The lights in the hall were out. In an ideal world the

maintenance staff would be on the job, heading for his floor in a team five strong. But in the everyday world Coe wanted to carry on inhabiting they'd be here next Tuesday at best, after daily harassment. One youth with a utility belt.

"What about Driscoll?"

". . . What about him?"

The sudden whine, the buzz.

"No no no what's the question? I'll answer, just tell me the—"

"Tearney told you to warn me off him?"

"Yes."

"How? What did she say?"

"She said he was—"

Oh God, he thought, oh God, what did she say? That he was not in the picture, That he was—

"—a person of interest, that's all. Not one of us. He's just someone who's made a success of himself—"

God, think, think. What had she said?

"—that he's been vetted for a gong. Both parties wooing him. And that's all. That's all."

"So he's hands off."

"Yes. That's what she said. That he's out of bounds. He's Do Not Disturb."

For a moment, the flat of the blade rested against Coe's cheek.

"If I decide Driscoll had anything to do with my son's death, do you seriously think telling me he's untouchable will have any effect?"

Coe swallowed.

"That was a question."

". . . No."

"And here's another one. Does Tearney believe that?"

"... I don't know."

"That doesn't surprise me."

Another silence. All JK Coe could hear was the ticking of a clock, which was running fast, and not a clock at all but his own heart.

There was a siren, somewhere, heading for a luckier emergency. But there was nobody coming for him.

And his own stink hung in the air. He'd never be rid of that. He could live through this evening, junk the carpet, scrub the walls for a week. And still he'd smell his own shit every time he sat quietly in this room.

Bettany said, "Off the books. Unofficial. A black-bag favour for a former comrade in arms. That's the size of it, right?"

"... Yes."

"If this turns out to be upside down ..."

Bettany was moving away now.

"... If it turns out you're using my son's death, and by you I mean you or Tearney or anyone else within ten miles of the Park, to put me into play ..."

JK Coe waited.

But there was no threat. There didn't need to be a threat.

Not after this.

The distant siren faded. Through the windows the lights of London would be blinking on and winking off, tracing the thousand stories he'd never know the ending of, nor ever want to. Right now all he wanted was to disappear into a hole of his own making, somewhere dark and safe, with no room for anyone but himself.

But the blade was back, its sudden electric whirr slicing his thoughts apart.

Bettany held it against his bound left hand and Coe tensed, yelped, and saw fingers falling to the floor, one little two little three little piggies, and his hand became a hunk of misshapen gristle.

I work in meat.

But the buzz clicked off as something fell loose, and Bettany withdrew behind him once more.

Afraid to speak, Coe flexed his fingers instead. The clothesline dropped away.

Very carefully, very slowly, Coe did nothing. Didn't rip himself free. Didn't jump to his feet, screaming.

Behind him a rustling, as if someone were getting dressed, ready to sneak into the night. The undoubted ending to so many of those other stories, winking and blinking away across London.

A click reached his ears, like the sound of a door being closed.

Coe waited but heard nothing else, other than what rose from the streets below, and his own breathing, and the too-fast ticking of his heart.

"Bettany?"

No reply.

"Are you still there?"

He'd seen this in a thousand movies, which always ended the same way. Best to stay still a while longer.

It was a full ten minutes before he rose at last, and let the clothesline puddle at his feet.

It was a good while longer before he stopped trembling.

3.4

Bettany dumped the high-vis tabard and clipboard in the first bin he came to. They were all he'd needed to gain access to Coe's building. *Problem with the electrics in the lobby, mate. Just come for a look-see.* Half the time nobody cared what your reason was, they'd buzz you in just to get you off their intercom. And anyone wanting further credentials could see he was here to work—the jacket, the clipboard.

The address had come courtesy of Bad Sam, who Bettany hoped never got to hear of this evening's work.

On Coe's landing he'd disconnected the overhead lights then worked Coe's lock with his brand-new toolkit, now dumped in the second bin he'd come to.

After that it was a matter of preparing the environment, and waiting for Coe to show up.

Bettany was on a bus now, upper deck. The streets were a dark carnival, people heading home, heading out, or settling in shop doorways with sheets of cardboard. He had slept rough a few times these past years. A life he'd fallen into without meaning it. When you cut all ties, you lost your choice of direction.

But his old life was reaching out to him. Ingrid Tearney . . . She was a penthouse operative, in and out of Whitehall, back and forth to DC, while he'd been a joe then briefly a Dog, jobs where you got your hands dirty. So why her interest?

Various answers suggested themselves. Things might, for instance, be as advertised, and to avoid having an ex-spook become a nuisance, Tearney was giving him Marten Saar on a plate. It made a certain sense. If he'd continued rattling cages in clubland Bettany would have attracted attention, and spies—even former spies—made for headline news, which the Service didn't like. And since the chances of him finding whoever'd actually sold Liam muskrat were non-existent, venting his anger on the big fish held definite appeal. So yes, it might be as simple as that.

Of course, Tearney might have her own reasons for wanting rid of Saar, in which case getting Bettany to pull the trigger would be a big win. It would explain why she'd used small-fry Coe, and kept everything off the books. Greenlighting murder, even of a drug dealer, wouldn't stand up to Cabinet scrutiny.

But targeting Saar left a loose end flapping. Source of London's muskrat or not, Marten Saar hadn't been there when Liam fell to his death. And somebody had been. The missing lighter proved that.

The bus, he registered, had been immobile for some time.

Even as he had the thought it pulled out into traffic. But given he'd spent the last hour torturing a member of the intelligence service, he should probably be more alert. If the Dogs were looking—if Coe had rung the alarm—he'd be downstairs at the Park before the bus was at the terminus.

Downstairs was where the hospitality suites were. Subtlety was never the Dogs' strong point.

But Coe had crapped himself, literally shit himself, in his

own sitting room. He'd been drenched with fear, slippery as a fish, gleaming in what little light there was. He wasn't going to sound the alarm. He'd go undercover instead, seal the memory off in a dark corner he'd try never to visit. Nobody would hear about it.

Except Tearney, Bettany thought. Coe would tell Tearney, and blame her for it too. He was a virgin, and she'd thrown him to the wolf. Tearney had to have known Bettany would need to verify her message, and that he'd go overboard to do so. Stripping naked, plugging in the knife—if Coe had been a veteran Bettany would have had to hurt him, but because he wasn't fear did all the work. Tearney had been around long enough to understand that. As of twenty minutes ago, Coe understood it too.

And Bettany himself, what did he know now that he hadn't known before?

That Coe had been telling the truth.

Or at least, believed he'd been telling the truth . . .

Because the other possibility was that Tearney was pointing him at Vincent Driscoll.

Time to get off, so he rang the bell, went downstairs, stepped onto another dark pavement. London swam into focus, familiar but strange at once. A video panel on a nearby litter bin streamed a live news channel, while over the road a Victorian lamp post's curves were ornate as a hatstand's. It was as if portals into the past, or the future, kept opening.

He wasn't being followed. No alarms had been rung. He spared a brief spasm of pity for JK Coe, and slipped off the thoroughfare and its limelight.

The other possibility was that Tearney was pointing him at Vincent Driscoll—why warn him off otherwise? A computer game designer didn't sound like a player, but computers got you places drugs never would. Maybe the games were a cover, and Driscoll was designing spyware.

In which case the picture flipped once more—now Driscoll was an asset, and Tearney really did want Bettany to keep his distance.

It was like holding a puzzle cube. He hadn't got it right yet. No answer left all sides the same colour.

He should sleep on it, but there was no chance of that. Forward momentum was needed. Into the dark streets he went.

3.5

It was a small shop and didn't look popular. Stationer's, it claimed. In the dusty window were colour-tinted plastic folders and a few reams of A4.

PHOTCOPIER NOT WORKING said a sign taped to the glass.

"Photocopier."

Bettany tried the door, which wouldn't open. But there was a light on, so he knocked. Waiting, he surveyed the street.

Hardly a street. An alley off a lane off a road off Cheapside. The shop's nearest neighbour was a pharmacist's offering three-for-two on sun-protection products, either eight months late or madly ahead of the curve.

He'd walked across the Millennium Bridge, halting on the gradient up to St. Paul's to look back at the dark water lapping its constant course. Maybe there, he thought—maybe, when this was over, he'd scatter Liam's ashes on the water. Every Londoner loved the river. Wasn't that right?

Every Londoner loved the river.

So maybe that was where he'd scatter Liam.

He banged the door again.

A shaggy-haired adolescent appeared, displaying his watch-face through the glass with a scowl.

Bettany pointed at the door handle.

With an elaborate sigh, the boy opened the door a crack.

"It's nearly seven, we're—"

"Dancer in?"

He thought for a moment he was too late. Wrong shop, wrong city, wrong year. But the boy pulled the door open and stood aside.

Bettany walked past him, past the weary stock of envelopes and adhesive notes, past the out-of-action "photocopier," to another door, this marked STAFF ONLY.

He didn't knock.

No windows, just a naked overhead bulb. It lit a cramped grubby office, mostly occupied by a desk, behind which sat a man, his face mostly occupied by spectacles.

"You're kidding me."

"Hello, Dancer."

"You are kidding me."

Bettany sat on the visitor's chair.

"Martin Boyd. As I live and breathe."

He waited.

"Though living and breathing," said Dancer, adjusting his glasses, "that is most definitely a temporary situation."

Dancer Blaine.

Dancer wasn't one of those names—Lofty, Brains—hilariously awarded in ill-fitting tribute. Dancer did in fact dance. An egg-cup-sized trophy, proudly displayed on his desk, attested to this fact. What he looked like doing it, or how he persuaded anyone to do it with him, remained profound mysteries. His grey-streaked hair was folded into a rope that hung down his back like a bellpull, and the eyes behind his thick round lenses were squirrely, hard and brown. It struck Bettany he was wearing the same clothes he'd worn last time he'd seen him, easily eight years ago.

Back when Bettany was Martin Boyd.

"I know people who'll be amazed you're still upright," Dancer went on. "Not been seen in years, you've not."

"Been away," Bettany said.

No trouble at all, he found his voice slipping into long dormant patterns. Like pulling a cover back over himself in the cold waste of the night.

A cover long blown, of course. They could stick it in the window next to those plastic folders, offer it for sale at a knockdown price. Buy one used identity, get a second one free.

Identities being among those things Dancer Blaine traded in.

Reams of A4, not so much.

"Not for as long as some of our mutual friends, you haven't. Fifteen to twenty, without so much as a goodbye. What with you giving your evidence behind a screen."

"I've always been a mite shy."

Dancer smiled with greasy teeth.

"Special Branch was it? SO11, or one of them?"

"One of them," Bettany agreed.

"And now the Brothers McGarry are pining for the open spaces."

"Sure they are," said Bettany.

He'd never laid eyes on the Brothers McGarry anywhere that didn't have a ceiling, a bar or a pole dancer in easy reach.

"Not to mention their old mates. Often ask about you, they do. You know, your whereabouts. That kind of thing."

"Hard as it is to fathom, I'm not here to chat about old times."

"Customer, is it? We've a deal on staplers this week."

"I'm fine for staplers."

"So what makes you think I'll help you?"

"You'd sell your family for twenty quid, Dancer. I'm pretty sure you'll help."

Dancer ran a hand across his scalp, looked at his palm, then wiped it on his trousers.

"Anything I might provide, don't you get that at work?"

"I've gone freelance."

"Gone rogue, more like. You've got the look. That's interesting."

"I'm glad you're entertained."

"Makes you more, what would be the word?"

"Here."

"I was thinking . . . vulnerable."

"You reckon?"

"Lacking back-up."

Bettany said, "Present company, Dancer, I need back-up like you need an emergency condom. You going to keep dreaming, or shall we get down to business?"

"What you after?"

"Handgun."

"Can't be done."

"Maybe I should have been clearer. I've just spent half an hour remodelling a colleague with a carving knife. It's taken it out of me, and I could do with a breather. So this is what's going to happen. You're going to cut out the sales chat and get down to business. Save me getting worked up again."

Dancer Blaine sneered, but not convincingly. He checked out Bettany's hands, his cuffs. Looking for stains.

"I clean up nice."

"What kind of handgun?"

"Any that works, that's here within the hour, suits me fine."

"Money."

"Two hundred."

"Ha!"

Bettany said nothing.

"Two hundred? You are joking me. You are positively, absolutely, pulling the chain."

Still nothing.

"For two hundred, I can maybe find you a potato gun. Not one that shoots potatoes, get me? One carved out of a potato but looks realistic. That do you?"

"You're forgetting your bonus."

"Oh, there's a bonus. That's good. Because I really appreciate a bonus, what with being so desperate for custom and all."

Bettany leaned forward.

"We both know you'll be on that phone, minute I'm out of here. Selling Martin Boyd to the highest bidder. To the Brothers McGarry, or their face on the streets. No shortage of candidates, is there? Price on my head, and all. You'll stand to pick up a nice slice of that, won't you?"

Dancer curled a lip.

"Picking up a slice of that whether I sell you a gun or not, old chum. Can't work that out, I'm not surprised you've had to go freelance."

"Well, that depends on you still being alive when I walk out of here, doesn't it? Old chum."

Dancer started to speak, then stopped. Ran a hand across his head again. Behind his bottle-glasses, squirrel eyes blinked three times in quick succession.

Bettany clasped his hands, and rested them on the desk in front of him.

He said, "Your boy through there's your runner, right?"

Dancer nodded, as Bettany had expected. No way would an old hand like Dancer Blaine keep merchandise on the premises.

"Well then."

He reached inside his coat pocket, and Dancer flinched.

"Two hundred," Bettany said.

The notes he put on the table were most of the rest of Liam's hoard.

Dancer looked at the money, then back at Bettany. There was calculation in his eyes, as well as fear and a splash of venom.

"Suppose it happens. Suppose you get your handgun. What's to stop you . . ."

"I have business elsewhere, Dancer. Make life difficult for me, and I'll get cross. Do what I want and I'll fade away."

His voice grew quieter.

"And once I've done that, you can start ringing round your mates. Can't you?"

Dancer studied the money again, licking it with his eyes.

Without shifting his gaze, he called out, "Get in here, Mose."

As if he'd been waiting behind the door, the shaggy-haired adolescent appeared.

3.6

An hour and forty minutes later, Bettany stood in a well-recessed shop doorway near Embankment, rain cracking off the arcade roof overhead. In his hand a carrier bag, and in the bag a shoebox.

It weighed more than his son. This thought wouldn't leave. It echoed to the patter of the raindrops.

There were bars along this stretch of road, and taxis cruising past. Not by any means a deserted part of the capital.

Dancer had given Mose whispered instructions, and sent him off to whatever lock-up, safe house or hole in the ground Dancer stashed his stock in. The shoebox he'd come back with held a Makarov, a Belgian model. Bettany had dry-fired it, there in Dancer's office. It didn't feel like it would blow his hand off when loaded.

He hadn't thought he'd ever hold a gun again. Had thought that part of his life was over.

A woman walked past, gave him a quick look, and hurried on.

What would Liam have said if he'd seen him tonight? Stark naked, wielding a carving knife? Threatening to lop parts off a man who'd never been more than a messenger?

It didn't matter. It wasn't relevant.

Liam was in an urn, a mess of grit and clinker.

Liam weighed less than a loaded gun.

More footsteps.

Bettany placed the bag at his feet.

He'd paid Dancer and walked riverwards, taking the back lanes, passing rows of restaurants and empty offices. Mose, trailing in his wake, was easy to spot. The kid was an unfinished article. That, or Dancer was too cheap to pay for quality.

The footsteps wavered slightly, but didn't stop.

He'd made no attempt to lose the boy until he'd reached Embankment station, slipping straight through from the riverside to the street beyond after a brief feint in the direction of the barriers. An amateur move, designed to make another amateur happy he'd not fallen for it. But Bettany had then immediately lost himself in a mid-evening jostle, leaving Mose at the station entrance, clueless.

Could have left it at that, thought Bettany. He could have faded away as promised. Mose wasn't going to find him. Dancer could tell anyone he liked that Martin Boyd was in town, but they'd need serious luck to track him down before he left. So there was no real call to do what he did next.

Which was step aside from the crowd, allowing Mose to see him.

Mose did. Mose would have had to be blind, drunk or both not to.

Next moment Bettany was back inside the crowd, and the moment after was in this quiet shop doorway, still wondering whether he'd have hurt Coe, if circumstances had demanded.

It didn't matter. Wasn't worth asking. Scaring him had been enough.

When Mose drew level Bettany pulled him in with one quick

yank on his arm, clamped his mouth shut with his free hand, and planted his knee firmly in the kid's crotch. He mapped the course of the boy's pain in the wide-open plains of his eyes, and waited until it reached its zenith before lowering him, quite gently, to the ground.

Then Bettany picked up his bag and walked on.

3.7

The shower passed, which made no difference to Dancer Blaine. Ensconced in his office, he hadn't known it was raining to start with. He'd simply sat until he was sure Martin Boyd had left, and Mose was on his tail, and then had stood, wrapped his arms around an imaginary friend, and glided round on the spot, imagination building a ballroom out of half a metre of carpet.

Glitterballs bloomed, an orchestra swelled, and bouquets were thrown by adoring crowds.

When Dancer was done he bowed low, doffed his glasses, and allowed his plait to graze the floor.

Then he sat back down and waited for the phone to ring.

There were a lot of ways of describing Dancer's principal line of business, but he liked to see it as making people up. Creating identities. He did other things too—the least of which was selling stationery, the worst handling guns—but making people up was what he did best. It wasn't far removed from what writers did, the difference being when you closed a book, the people stopped existing.

The people Dancer made up could thrive for the rest of their naturals, if they didn't do anything stupid.

The chief stupidity was and always had been drawing attention to yourself.

When the phone rang at last it was Mose, to say he'd lost Boyd, or Boyd had lost him. Dancer wasn't surprised. Whatever else he was Boyd was a professional, while Mose was basically Work Experience.

He hung up then dialled a number he knew by heart.

"It's Dancer," he said. "The man in?"

He waited, listened, lit a cigarette.

"Yeah, this number," he said. "I'll wait."

He cradled the phone and coughed out smoke.

The shelving opposite blurred, wobbled, then resumed its previous position.

Mose had lost Martin Boyd around the Embankment, which meant the Embankment was nowhere near Boyd's hidey hole. But that was okay. Where Boyd's hidey hole was was somebody else's problem. The fact that he had one was all Dancer was currently selling.

Someone like Martin Boyd, you didn't expect a second crack at. He was Security, or from one of those police squads sounded like a postcode or a junk-food additive. S06, EC11, whatever. They came in undercover and did their job, and your window for wreaking personal justice upon them was brief, because after your arrest you couldn't mess with them. For a start they'd generally vanished off the face of the earth. But even if they hadn't, targeting them was an act of war. Might as well dig your own hole, plant a headstone, and wait. Because undercover types didn't play by their own rules, they played by yours. And you didn't want a level playing field when the opposition were trained in use of weapons, rather than just in possession of a hooky firearm.

What was interesting about Boyd, though, was a hooky firearm was exactly what he'd been after.

Dancer spat noisily into, very nearly, his wastepaper basket.

Not that Martin Boyd was his real name.

The possibility was, of course, that Boyd was just bread on the water, deliberately giving the impression he was out of the game. There were some sharp buggers out there, and Dancer wouldn't put it past them to use an old hand as bait, see who came to the surface. If that was what was happening things were likely to get noisy, and it might be sound politics to take an early break, Portugal or somewhere, until the dust settled.

Boyd hadn't smelled like Job, though.

On the other hand, if he'd smelled like Job last time round, the Brothers McGarry wouldn't be out of the picture.

Dancer killed his cigarette.

Bottom line was, what Boyd had done to the Brothers McGarry would have happened sooner or later anyway—it, or something like. They'd have been picked up for a dodgy tail light in a van match-ready for D-Day, or hosed out of their cars by a rival on the fringes of Epping Forest. Six of one and the same of the other, far as Dancer was concerned. Because if it wasn't the Brothers McGarry it would be someone else, and here was your proof—the brothers were banged up, and guess what? Gun crime hadn't gone anywhere. Gun crime was still edging up the charts, gaining on Possession With Intent, and muttering dark nothings about Grievous Bodily Harm.

So no, Dancer didn't care what Boyd had done, and wasn't even especially aggrieved that the man had threatened him, here in his own office. Threats, actual pummellings even, went with the territory. You simply made a mental note, and waited for the wheel to turn. It wasn't personal. It was just the way business was done.

In this particular instance, the wheel was turning faster than usual, of course.

The phone rang, and Dancer uncradled the receiver.

Sometimes you made people up. Sometimes you sold them.

Either way, the wheel kept turning.

He said, "You'll never guess who I just had in the shop."

3.8

The man Dancer Blaine had called The Man otherwise went by Bishop. He too had known Martin Boyd in a previous life, and even if he hadn't would have been keen to hear of his reappearance, the way any local businessman might rub his hands on hearing word of a tourist.

Tourists were there to be fleeced.

When this happened to tourists, it was often a metaphor.

On the table in front of Bishop was a photograph, one from that previous life. These days you'd do it on a phone, but not so many phones had cameras back then, and he'd used one of those yellow disposables. The occasion had been a party, everyone drunk, Bishop included, which must have been why he'd thought photos a good idea. Photography was generally frowned on in these circles, photos being not so much keepsakes as evidence.

The party had been for the Brothers McGarry and Bishop's picture showed the pair of them, each with an arm round the man in the middle, Martin Boyd, friend, trusted lieutenant, who'd personally sourced a bent quartermaster in Herefordshire, a triumph netting a supply of weaponry officially destined for destruction, so more than deserving of the man-hug he was enjoying. Bishop did a quick mental calculation, and as it was one he'd made before, was reasonably sure his answer was accurate. Four months and seventeen days. The picture had been taken four months and seventeen days before the Brothers McGarry, along with everyone who'd ever so much as passed them the salt, had been arrested.

Trusted lieutenant. Snake in the grass.

Bishop himself had gone down for five, been out in three and a half. As for the Brothers McGarry, they were walled up for a sizeable chunk of forever, but that didn't mean they lacked influence.

More importantly, it didn't mean they'd run out of money.

And they had some very specific ideas about how they'd like it spent.

With a pair of scissors Bishop carefully cut the photograph into three strips, and held the middle section up for a better look.

He'd be older now. He'd have a new name. But what was interesting was he didn't seem to have changed his appearance—hadn't changed his hair, wasn't using coloured contacts. Had wandered into Dancer Blaine's place as if he didn't give a damn.

What was even more interesting was that he was out on his own.

Back in the day, Bishop reckoned, Boyd had been MI5—not an organisation to get messy with. If he was still with them, the Brothers McGarry's money was likely to remain unspent. Because if you tried to collect on the head of a cop you were looking to get dead, no two ways about it, but do the same with a spook, and dead might look an attractive option. Those guys could disappear you. But if Dancer Blaine was right, Boyd was not only back on the streets but unprotected.

Bad news for him. The Brothers McGarry had had years to think up what needed doing to Boyd—they hadn't so much put a price on his head as itemised his body. There were strict instructions about getting it on film. They'd watch it on phones, in their cells. Help pass the time.

One little strip of photo.

Bishop would have two thousand copies on the street inside the hour.

Bettany thought of heading home, but only long enough that the word flared brightly for half a second—*home*—before burning into darkness, like a filament briefly glanced at, and scorched into the retina. Liam's home. Not his.

Not Liam's either now, though Liam was still in occupation. Bettany had left the urn of ashes on the kitchen table, like an item of shopping waiting to be packed away. Because where did you put something like that? Anywhere you put it, it felt like you carried it still.

Same weight, different burden.

He'd ditched the shoebox, and carried the gun in his coat pocket. It gave him the kind of lopsided look policemen were trained to watch for, but that couldn't be helped. The rain had eased and he was crossing the river again, not because he needed to but because he had to keep moving. That was the current plan. He couldn't go back to the flat. He didn't think Coe would have sounded the alarm, but if he had, that was the first place the Dogs would look.

Lights flickered up and down the Thames. A small boat's cabin was lit like a candle in the dark.

He thought, *I need to eat.* See the evening out—it was barely nine. Then find somewhere to put his head down for a few hours.

Tomorrow, he'd start putting things straight.

Hands in pockets, he headed for Waterloo.

"The railway stations. No, not the stations themselves, the doss-houses round them. Yes, and the hostels. King's Cross especially. And Paddington, and right, yeah, Liverpool Street. Waterloo. Other than that, you know the score. The usual bars, west and east. Anywhere there's a good evening crowd, but one with regulars, get me? Don't bother with the tourist haunts. Round Hoxton way, yeah, course. You going to just run through the bloody A to Z, wait for me to say yeah, no? You've done this before, right? . . . Yes, it's important. Would I be wasting my time if it wasn't? Swear to God, I sometimes wonder why I don't just swap you for a trained . . . iguana. What? Iguana. It's a kind of lizard—look, just get it done. I want the city papered, and I want this bleeder traced. And I want it soon. I want you ringing back so fast you're on call waiting before I've hung up. Got it?"

Bishop ended the call and took a deep breath.

Then he made another one.

3.9

There are a lot of threads in the city. Pull enough of them and you can see the pavements twitch.

In his cubbyhole of an office even Dancer Blaine knew that. Part of it was the still-fizzing energy of having had the actual walking Martin Boyd in his shop, and part of it was knowing that by calling Bishop, he'd set wheels in motion no bugger could halt.

While another part, only just starting to bite, was the awareness that if Boyd disappeared without trace now, if he sank from view like a stone in the Thames, then he, Dancer, was going to be facing some very awkward questions . . .

And Bishop himself could feel it, but then he was doing the pulling—all those copies of that celluloid strip, a phone number printed beneath, had come rolling out of a copier, stacking up in reams that were dispatched as soon as ready, finding their way into the hands of dozens of boys, dozens of girls, rounded up by what was left of the Brothers McGarry's network. And meanwhile the same image was bouncing through the ether, jumping from iPhone to iPhone, every contact reached for, thread linking to thread, knotting together, forming a net to drop over London's nightlife.

The railway stations. King's Cross especially. And Paddington, and right, yeah, Liverpool Street. Waterloo.

And the clubs and bars, though nowhere Boyd had ever hung in the old days, nowhere the Brothers McGarry were still mourned or celebrated, which ruled out the further reaches of the East End . . .

See? Already the city was growing smaller, as if these threads Bishop was pulling were attached to London's corners, so everything not nailed down tumbled into one small area where the searchers waited, the searchers being anyone who could look at a photo, recognise a face, and dial a number.

Next to which Bishop had printed, in bold, *££££*.

In a hard-luck café, one of those linoleum-floored check-table-clothed outfits that were rarer by the year, Tom Bettany had gone to ground. Cup of tea in front of him, empty plate with its sheen of congealing grease pushed to one side.

He'd had a sudden memory of an evening in a café not unlike this, back in Marseilles. With Majeed and a few others, and there'd been wine and beer of course, not cups of tea, and the food hadn't come swaddled in grease, and there hadn't been tomato-shaped plastic bottles on the table . . . Come to think of it, it had been nothing like this, except inasmuch as it had been near a travellers' hub, with long-distance coaches growling past the window every few minutes.

Bettany waited, but nothing more of that memory came back. It was simply a flash from the past, a light switched on and off in another room. And it troubled him that there was no less weight to this random slice of his history than there was to any other memory he had, of Liam, of Hannah, or of edgier times, times when he'd had to suppress his real self . . . His past was a collage of different identities, none of them realer than any other.

And none, in the end, walked away from.

What was real, what had weight, was what he had to do tomorrow.

A boy walked past the window, bobble hat lopsided on his head, a sheet of paper scrolled in his hand, his face a brief smudge against a noisy background. Homeless, Bettany could tell. There was always something in the face. He'd seemed in a hurry, headed towards Waterloo. Everyone had a mission. Everyone had somewhere they needed to be, an undercover self, urging them on.

Bettany paid for his meal and left, had a quick internal debate about heading for the station himself and hopping on a tube, and decided not to. Railway stations were best avoided.

On foot, he headed for the bridge.

The weary expression Ralph wore wasn't exclusive to the small hours, but by the time they rolled around he had an excuse. In old-time songs, bartenders wiped glasses while listening to a man in a hat pour his sorrows out. They'd dispense wisdom in return for a mighty tip. The worst they'd suffer was an out-of-tune piano scoring the heartbreak.

In real life, the nearest Ralph got to dispensing wisdom was explaining where the toilets were to the same drunk for the third time. And that you couldn't smoke in here. By two he'd have sold a kidney to hear an accordion, let alone a piano. Anything to put an end to the pitiless club beat, the sound of meat being tenderised. Some mornings, lying in bed, he could feel it in the soles of his feet. It didn't make him want to dance. It made him want to saw himself off at the ankles.

There must be easier ways to make a living.

Tonight there was a healthy crowd, if "healthy" suited a mass of kids so bent on self-destruction. The amount of booze they put away would shame a Catholic priest. Ralph had a headache from the noise and what felt like tendon damage from pouring drinks, the repetitive strain of jamming glass against optic, twisting cap from bottle. No one was telling him sorrows, but everyone was giving him grief. Nearest he'd had to a break tonight was a single smoke round back, resting against the wall.

Someone was waving something at him down the bar.

Like any good barman Ralph had the ability to make a queue in his head from the crowd in front of him, so he served three others before he reached that part of the bar, and the waving girl had disappeared by then. Where she'd been standing was a sheet of paper, a flyer it looked like, with a narrow strip of photograph copied onto it.

Underneath that a phone number, and underneath that ££££.

Some new form of stealth advertising, he thought. An on-the-fly way of attracting punters. Tell 'em there's money in it, because that always works. But there was always money in it and the money never materialised, that was the mystery. And even when it did it was gone in the morning, like something from a fairytale.

Ralph could have told the girl all this if she'd still been there, but because she wasn't, he had to settle for telling himself.

He scrunched the paper into a ball and lobbed it at the bin below the bar.

Bettany found himself back near the Angel, having walked clear up from the Thames, the city's nightlife flashing past in cabs and cars and buses, or rumbling underground when he crossed one of the thin patches, spaces where the subterranean made itself felt. His hands in his pockets, the right one curled comfortably round the Makarov—comfortably was the word, the handle moulded to fit. Dancer Blaine would have long since spread the word of his reappearance. All that nightlife in cabs and cars and buses, some of it would be responding to texts and emails by now, an equivalent to the police's be-on-lookout-for. Twitches on threads. Bettany was under no illusions about how badly they'd want him, the Brothers McGarry and their clan, and had a pretty shrewd idea they wouldn't have a swift exit planned either. But then, Bettany didn't plan to be around much longer. They'd have to be extraordinarily good, or extraordinarily lucky, to get a fix on his whereabouts within the next twenty-four hours.

By then, he'd know the truth about what had happened to Liam.

Rolling over in his mind, like a ball caressed by a bowler, were the names of Vincent Driscoll, Marten Saar.

It was clearing-out time before Ralph noticed the ball of paper on the floor. Not remembering what it was he unscrewed it, glanced at the photo, and was about to reverse the process, finding the damn bin this time, when something tugged at him, a tremor of recognition.

The photo showed a sliver of a man flanked by two others, whose images had been excised. It was black and white and looked old—not *old* old, but old. And the man, his face—it was the man from the other night, he was sure of it. Almost sure. The man who'd been looking for his son. He'd done some miles since the photo was taken, and grown a lot of hair, but if you took away the beard and general shagginess, Ralph thought you could see the same man, the same eyes staring back at you. His eyes had been blue, which a black-and-white couldn't show of course, but in the same way he knew the photo was old, Ralph knew this man's eyes were blue.

Beneath the photo a phone number, and a little row of pound signs, ££££.

He'd given the man his twenty quid back, he remembered that. A man who looked like he'd been sleeping on park benches, but had money to throw at bartenders who might have served his son. Ralph had returned his money because he looked like he needed it more, and besides, he was carrying his son's ashes in a bag. That's what he'd said, anyway. You had to assume he wasn't entirely there—making a nuisance of himself for streets around, crashing clubs and bars.

That was the same night two doormen had their kneecaps sorted in an alley. If not for that, this guy would have been the week's main topic.

Everyone had seen him. Everyone would be seeing this, too, the flyer left on Ralph's bar. And if he'd spotted the resemblance, so would someone else—it was just a matter of waiting for the pennies to drop—and then the number would be rung, and questions asked and answered.

££££

He'd felt sorry for the guy, sure. But somebody was going to collect, and Ralph had already turned money down once.

He checked the place was empty, then reached for the phone.

3.10

"So you'd be Ralph."

"Yeah."

"Ralphie. What've you got for me, Ralphie?"

"It's like I just said to your man there—"

"Yeah, but you're talking to me now. Just tell me what you have to say."

Pause.

"I don't even know who I'm talking to."

"You can call me Bishop."

Pause.

"Name rings a bell, does it?"

"I've heard of you, yeah. I reckon."

"You reckon. That's good. You just keep on reckoning that, Ralphie. And meanwhile, tell me what you know."

"I serve bar."

Pause.

"Nothing to be ashamed of there, Ralphie, but let's cut to the chase, shall we? You serve bar where."

"Place called Kings of Cool."

"Hoxton way?"

"Yeah."

"So you serve bar in Hoxton and·you're calling me because you saw my number on a flyer. Do you know the man, Ralphie?"

"No."

"But you've seen him around."

"Yeah. I think so."

"When?"

"He had more hair, though. A beard and that. Looked like he'd been sleeping rough."

"When?"

"Couple of nights ago?"

"You asking or telling?"

"Couple of nights ago."

"Rough sleeper, how come he's finding his way into a bar round N1?"

"He slipped past the doormen."

"He slipped past the doormen. You wouldn't be pulling my chain, would you, Ralphie?"

"It's what happened."

"What name'd he give?"

"He didn't."

"Course not, rough sleeper, finessing his way past a couple of Hoxton's finest. What'd he drink?"

"He didn't get a drink."

"So he was what, just checking out the décor, Ralphie?"

"He had a photo. He was trying to find out . . ."

Pause.

"Getting bored here, Ralphie."

"He had a bag with him. A cloth bag. And an urn in it . . . He said it was his son. His son's ashes."

Pause.

"You're pulling my chain."

"He had a photo too. Wanted to know if I recognised his son. If he was a regular. He'd been up and down the road, asking in all the clubs. Made himself well unpopular."

"I bet he did an' all, Ralphie. I bet he did."

Pause.

"Okay, Ralphie. Your place doesn't do cabaret, does it?"

". . . Once in a blue moon."

"Because if you're making that lot up, you really should be on a stage. Son's ashes in a bag. That is . . ."

Pause.

"Pinteresque."

Pause.

"He wrote plays. Never mind. Kings of Cool. This pans out, there'll be someone popping in, Ralphie, see you right."

Bishop hung up.

Afterwards Ralph washed his hands, aware he didn't really need to. He'd washed them once already, and nobody got dirty hands just using the phone.

Still.

He washed them anyway.

Bishop didn't know what that was about, the stuff with the ashes in the bag, but it didn't matter, not at four o'clock in the morning. So Martin Boyd was having some sort of meltdown, but who cared? Meltdowns made you careless. Boyd must have known getting hold of a gun was going to light up the switchboard of his old acquaintance. He had to be off his nut going to Dancer Blaine to get tooled up.

Though maybe, he thought, Boyd was on some kind of quest. A dead boy in one hand, a gun in the other, yeah, some kind of quest. That would be where the gun came in.

But it didn't matter. Made no difference to what Bishop was going to do next, which was summon up some muscle and put it on the streets of N1. Maybe Boyd would get lucky, and see his quest through before they picked him up. If not, unfinished business would be the least of his worries. He'd be starring in his very own snuff movie, scripted by the Brothers McGarry. All Bishop had to do was set it up.

With just a few more twitches on these threads.

PART FOUR

■ ■ ■

4.1

Twenty-two storeys buys a lot of Hackney.

What it bought Marten Saar was an almost uninter-rupted view of rooftops, terraced houses and shorter blocks of flats, of pubs and sports centres, shops and office complexes, garages and schools. Trees too, and snatches of water, roads everywhere, and housing estates. The cars and buses he could see were Dinky-sized. The people shuffling around the estates weren't even that. At this time of morning they were pale grey shadows wafting homewards. Ghosts.

This block, Saar's, was the easternmost of a row of three, so he got to watch the sun struggle up, little more than a silver disc today, a dying light bulb behind a gauze curtain.

A sky the colour of dishrags.

Stifling, here on the twenty-second floor.

Which was not like the other floors in this block or its neigh-bours. To arrive was to find the flats' front doors barred over, steel shutters pulled down, and scraps of tape the wasp-striped colour of crime scenes dangling from handles. Only one door was unob-structed, and it led into this huge room, an L-shape with irregularly spaced windows which had once let light into different flats, and walls which changed colour every few metres, and a mosaic of different carpets, none quite joining up. The inverse L, the space's interlocking letter, comprised a mish-mash of bedrooms, dormitories and workspace, where product was bagged into saleable quantities. At any given moment, the flat contained upwards of fifty kilos of controlled substances.

A lot of jailtime to keep on a floor with few exits.

That was what Kask said. Oskar Kask, his own right hand.

"We get raided, we're none of us going anywhere. Unless you're in the mood for a hard landing."

Oskar had stood shoulder-to-shoulder with him during the lean years, broken legs when legbreaking was needed, but had lately taken to saying things like *Sure, boss?* when he should have been saying *Sure, boss.*

He trusted Oskar with his life. But trust needed daily renewal.

Saar wasn't worried about surprises. You didn't put a police team together without disturbing the pool, and the ripples would reach him long before the motors arrived—he'd spread enough money around to make sure of that. The product would be in an unoccupied flat downstairs way ahead of any doors being kicked in.

Police aside, the twenty-second floor wasn't reached easily. While there were pairs of lifts in each corner of the towerblock, seven were piss-stinking boxes of filth, their walls so scarred by burnmarks, so obsessively scribbled on, that stepping inside was like climbing into a stalker's head. Only the eighth lift moved without squeak or rattle, and this was guarded night and day by one of Saar's men, on the off-chance someone who didn't know the rules wandered in, wanting to use it. A visitor from out of town, say. A Martian.

All of which should have made him feel secure, but success carried its own burdens. The trust thing for one. The daily renewal it required. Oskar at his shoulder like he'd always been but dropping questions into his ear now, like *Isn't it time we consolidate our market area?* Oskar could see the future falling into place, like a jigsaw completed by an invisible hand.

He claimed it would require only a small war.

That's why they needed the Cousins' Circle.

Saar hadn't slept. A pale rake with a permanent five o'clock shadow and eyes like pocket calculators, he didn't sleep much. Nights were for business, holding court in a roped-off West End club—the second best use of a velvet rope was to keep losers at bay. Saar did deals, took meetings, explored ways of shifting product. Every ounce of muskrat, the hippest strain of cannabis currently sedating the city, passed through his fingers. This monopoly was down to two things, supply and trend. The source was one Saar had cultivated for years, but he'd got lucky with the second, and everyone knew it. The thing about trends was, the clue was in the name. Blink twice and something else would come along, and muskrat would be history.

This is why we need to consolidate, Oskar said. *Now.*

Truth to tell, Oskar had a point. They'd never be in a stronger position, and once they got weaker, they could end up being consolidated themselves.

Market pressure. One of the headaches business involved.

Getting in bed with the Cousins' Circle, though, that made him uneasy. No wonder he was pacing the floor at this hour, flicking through seventy-five channels on a plasma screen, looking for nothing in particular, and not finding it.

Elsewhere on the twenty-second, others had no trouble sleeping. There were seven of his guys in their room and a pair of girls in his own, though he'd mostly watched and smoked. Marlboro, not product. He was lighting one now as a door opened, and he turned to see Oskar Kask, buttoning his shirt, yawning, rubbing his head with the knuckles of his right hand.

You expected sparks when he did that.

Oskar said, "You're up early."

"I don't sleep. You know that."

"Worried about the meet?"

That was something else Marten Saar had noticed lately. Oskar, others too, but mostly Oskar, saying things like *meet* when they meant *meeting*. All that effort put into learning English, so fluent they spoke it among themselves, and for what? So they could start getting it wrong on purpose. Saar blamed the TV.

He switched it off.

"Should I be?"

"Nah, boss. It'll go like a dream."

"Because we have such a great history together."

Oskar Kask beetled, then unbeetled, brows.

"The thing about history, Marten, is it's over. That's why they call it history."

He wasn't tall, Oskar Kask, but made up for it in energy. Even now, three minutes out of bed, it fizzed in him. He kept his hair short because it grew in tight little corkscrews, but Saar had always seen that as just another way Oskar's inner electricity escaped. His beard came flecked with grey, like Saar's own, but Oskar's was heavier. It looked like he had three days' worth, and he'd shaved yesterday.

"And these guys, they're all business. You know that."

He knew that, as much as anyone knew anything about the Cousins' Circle, which was Russian-based, multiethnic, multinational, and enjoyed the double charm of having its existence doubted as much as its reach was feared.

"Besides. Join the Circle and we don't have to worry about muskrat going out of fashion because we'll have a lock on whatever the next big thing is too. This is good business, Marten. The Circle, they're Google. They're Apple. You don't want to go head to head with them. You want to stand shoulder to shoulder."

"And while we are standing shoulder to shoulder," said Marten Saar, "who will be watching our backs?"

"That's not how this'll go. They don't want us out of the game, they want us to be their team on the ground. Distribution. Goodwill. All that shit. You know?"

"You're a good friend, Oskar."

"I try to be."

"And I know you think this is best."

"It's the way forward, Marten."

"But if I decide they're playing a double game, looking to ease us out of the picture . . ."

"We walk away."

"We do."

It was almost on his tongue to add drama—*And we burn them where they stand*, something like that, something else from TV. But it would have been worse than drama, would have been bravado. To utter threats would have been the little boy boasting that he wasn't scared of wolves, because he wasn't in a forest. But wolves had a way of bringing the forest with them. It didn't matter where you were. It was where they were that counted.

You're a good friend, Oskar. It was true. And it was also true he'd never been an ideas man, more an enforcer—all that energy had to go somewhere. Reliably vicious, but never a thinker. Yet here he was, brokering their common future.

It was a good plan. A dangerous plan, because if trust needed daily renewal, trusting Russians was a minute-by-minute affair, but still, it was a good plan because if it worked, their future was secure and their competition was dead.

If it worked.

Whether it was the danger or the hope he couldn't tell, but one or the other lit a thrill inside Marten Saar. He remembered the girls in his bed, asleep but wakeable. Maybe he'd more than watch this time.

He said to Oskar, "I'm going back to bed," and padded out of the L-shaped room, gown flapping at his knees.

Leaving Oskar Kask lighting a cigarette with a blue plastic lighter, and watching the sun attempt to make an impression on the streets below.

4.2

Morning rose to the surface like trapped gas. At the tube station the crowd dispersed as if expecting random sniper fire. A little behind the first surge, Dame Ingrid Tearney crested the steps and joined the pavement procession.

Lights changed. Traffic snarled.

It was another damp day, vapour clouding every pane of glass, the sky an impenetrable grey bowl upended over the city. Overcoats and umbrellas shielded bodies. Hoods obscured faces.

Dame Ingrid, ash-blonde this morning, paused to adjust her gloves, holding them at the wrist and flexing her fingers one by one. Then continued on her way.

A figure stepped in front of her as a bus swept past.

She might have been expecting him.

"You look a mess."

He felt one.

JK Coe had spent the night bundling reams of ripped-up black plastic bags into a giant ball he then disposed of via the stairs—the lift was too enclosed a space, too inviting of assault. In the basement by the bins he'd frozen, petrified by a noise he couldn't identify. Any other night he'd have shrugged it off. Londoners are used to rats. But he'd had his foundations rocked, and everything was a threat.

Once he'd dared move he'd found his clothes in a pile on his bedroom floor, wallet and watch on top, as if abandoned on a beach by a man faking his own death. So today there was a new, reborn JK Coe. This one wore a blue cagoule and jeans ripped at the knee. He'd showered twice but slime still oozed from his pores, coating his body in a paste that was two parts shame, one part fear.

"You'd better walk with me."

Nobody paid attention because there was nothing to see. It might have been a son joining his mother, or a Samaritan offering a rough-sleeper breakfast.

A street-sweeping lorry bustled past tight to the kerb, rearranging gutter grime with its brushes' circular motion. They waited until it, and the frustrated queue of cars behind it, was past and half-scuttled across the road, Dame Ingrid somehow making the scuttle dignified, or at least plausible.

Smaller streets awaited, passages between towers of glass and concrete. The traffic noise abated but other sounds took its place, rumblings and groanings, snatches of music, the wasplike buzz of a helicopter. Rounding a corner, they passed the entrance to a car park. A woman with a dog was scooping shit into a small blue bag.

These details tumbled round Coe's mind. It was like recovering from illness, or slowly becoming less drunk. Everything strange and familiar at once.

"So Bettany came for you?"

Something about the question, the way it dropped from her fully formed, threw a switch in his head.

". . . You knew he would."

"It seemed likely."

This stated as a matter of fact, as if it were absurd of him to have considered otherwise.

"You should have warned me!"

She halted abruptly, and gave him a look so sharp it ought to have had a handle on one end.

"You've had an upsetting experience. But address me in that tone again, Mr. Coe, and there will be repercussions. Do I make myself clear?"

". . . Yes."

"An apology would not go amiss."

". . . I'm sorry."

She blinked regally. Which evidently qualified as acceptance, for having done so, she resumed their stately progress.

"There seemed no need to warn you," she said. "You're Psych Eval. Junior, granted, but nevertheless. Psych Eval. One would have thought you'd have spared a moment to consider the possible ramifications of your meeting with Bettany."

"All I was doing was delivering a message!"

The exclamation mark earned him another sharp look.

"And all he was doing was verifying its content."

And then she sighed, a faint wisp of noise. Wearing Anna Valentine today, not that JK Coe would have recognised it. If he had, he might also have registered that it was neither last year's collection nor the previous year's, but the one before that.

"Our Mr. Bettany," she said, "has played both sides of the field. He's been undercover, and he's been a Dog. Which means he has a tendency to treat all unknowns as hostiles and all information as a lie. It was never likely he'd take delivery of a message at face value. You can't have failed to be aware of that."

"It didn't occur to me he'd . . ."

"Yes?"

He said nothing.

An ambulance rumbled past, in no great hurry.

Dame Ingrid said, "What did you tell him?"

"I didn't tell him anything."

"Mr. Coe, of one thing I am absolutely certain, and that is that you'd have answered any question he put to you. So, again. What did you tell him?"

"Nothing. I mean, nothing I hadn't already told him. Because I don't know anything, do I? All I was doing was repeating what you told me. And that was all true, wasn't it?"

"Of course it was, dear boy."

He'd come to confront her because he'd been through hell, and no way could he vent that on the one responsible—in his imagination he could take Bettany apart with a chainsaw, but reality wasn't going to cooperate. So he'd come seeking Dame Ingrid instead, but was no longer sure what he'd expected. An apology? An admission that the message he'd given Bettany had a coded element beyond his understanding? But instead she was calling him *dear boy* again.

Even that ambulance had made him flinch, and it hadn't been keening. Was just another vehicle negotiating the streets.

He wondered how long he'd be jumping at shadows.

"I thought he was going to kill me."

Words he hadn't known he'd been about to say.

"But he didn't."

"And what would you have done if he had?"

"My dear boy, I'd have been most seriously distressed."

Nothing in her tone suggested otherwise.

"And what would have happened to Bettany?"

Which provoked another sigh.

"Mr. Coe, you do understand the concept of the greater good?"

"You said this wasn't an op."

"And it isn't. But Thomas Bettany remains an ex-member of our Service. Now," and here she leaned closer to him in the manner of a teacher about to unveil a basic rule, one to stand him in good stead ever after, "we've had quite enough bad publicity in recent years as a result of Service boys embroiling themselves in squalid little scrapes. It doesn't look good. It doesn't look good at all."

It didn't. JK Coe wasn't about to dispute that.

"So if he'd killed you we'd have had to sweep it under the carpet. You'd have been a random victim of city crime, Mr. Coe. But you'd have caused no embarrassment to us, and I'd have been proud of you for that."

Well, at least that was an honest response.

She said, "As it is, advising Bettany to lay off Vincent Driscoll could only ever have had two possible outcomes. One, that he would lay off Vincent Driscoll. An unlikely outcome, but not entirely beyond the bounds of possibility. Or two, that he would take this as an indication that Vincent Driscoll was in fact responsible for what happened to his son, and act accordingly. Very much not what we wanted. But having paid you his little visit—"

(His little visit. As if dropping in for a cup of tea.)

"—he now knows there was no stratagem involved, which makes it far more likely that he'll do what we want him to do. And lay off Vincent Driscoll."

Coe said, "So torturing me was a necessary part of the process. As you'd planned it."

A sigh.

"Mr. Coe, why did you join the Service?"

Wrongfooted, he stammered nonsense. Sense of duty, desire to serve.

"In which case, you can be satisfied with last night's work. You do understand the essential nature of what has happened, don't you?"

"I—"

"All the same, I'll spell it out. The essential nature of what has happened is that it remains classified. You do not speak of it. To anyone. And if you ever again accost me in this fashion, you will learn the meaning of power. Is that clear?"

He allowed that it was.

"Good. Now go home, Mr. Coe. You don't look yourself. We all need a sick day now and then."

And just like that, dismissed, he was adrift in Central London.

Dame Ingrid carried on alone. Within the minute she'd produced a mobile, and came to a halt near the cobbled entrance to a mews. Whoever she called answered on the first ring.

She said, "I think we can expect Bettany to make a move soon. Keep an eye on him."

Out of nowhere a sparrow appeared, and began a minute examination of a space between two stones.

"Some kind of low-level torture, apparently. Nothing too serious. The young man was reluctant to go into detail, which I expect means he disgraced himself."

Finding a crumb, the sparrow speared it with its beak.

"I assume he'll go home and try to put it behind him. But either way, we can tidy up later."

She ended the call.

The sparrow flew away.

4.3

From the top deck of the bus, Flea Pointer looked out on the usual chaos.

Once in a while, you find yourself engaged in that pavement dance in which both partners step aside in the same direction, then correct themselves, then do it again ... It generally ends with amused apology on both sides. Viewed from above, what was amazing was that you rarely got head-on collisions, that fist-fights weren't breaking out. Instead, what Flea was watching resembled a physics experiment in which particles rushed around at great speed and in great proximity, only their innate tendency to repel their like ensuring they never touched.

Something about which thought inevitably led to Vincent.

Not touching was a thing with Vincent Driscoll, of course, and that wasn't just about physics, wasn't just about the physical. She sometimes wondered if he even remembered who she was from day to day. Oh, he had a grasp of her name, and her function—to keep the human elements of the business ticking over without his having to get involved—but all he needed for that was a Post-it on his fridge. *The woman you see at work is Flea*

Pointer. She deals with the people. One quick glance at breakfast, and he'd be up to speed. And while at first she had regarded this with an amusement not untinged with contempt, over the past year it had come to seem less funny, and that slight contempt had turned inward. What did it say about her, that he had so little interest? Zero interest.

Nothing. She found she was mouthing the word aloud, and disguised this by mouthing another word or two, as if humming a lyric or rehearsing a shopping list, then glanced around to see who was staring at the mad lady. But nobody was staring at the mad lady. Everyone had their own bubble they were trying not to burst.

But nothing. That was what it said about her. Vincent was Vincent, and Flea Pointer could be . . . Kylie Minogue, it wouldn't make a difference. Talk about being inside your own bubble. Vincent, famously, had written *Shades* in his teenage bedroom, and to all purposes he was in there still, building it anew each morning. Boo Berryman aside, he didn't have close relationships, and he was only close to Boo so Boo could keep everyone else away. Throwing around words like Asperger's was a cliché—the slightest indication of indifference, and onlookers started clucking about where you fell on the spectrum. And that went tenfold if you worked in IT. So it would be easy to write Vincent off as someone for whom intimate relationships were like trying to breathe on the moon, but Flea thought, had always thought, that the truth lay elsewhere. That all that was really needed was for someone to find the key to his bedroom door, and let him out.

Here was her stop. Abandoning her survey of the city's mad dance, she made her way down the stairs and joined it briefly, before leaving the pavement for the towpath, and heading for Lunchbox.

Today, she had not thought about Liam until leaving her flat. She thought about him now, though, about the little hole his absence would make in her day. Soon she would have to raise the matter with Vincent, in fact. Talk about recruitment. Though she had the feeling that this wasn't going to happen, that Liam didn't need replacing because Liam had been the gimmick hire, a phrase she couldn't swear to anyone having used, yet which had seemed to hang in the air somehow. Liam had been a sweet guy, but he wouldn't have been there if he hadn't been the first one to play *Shades* properly. Something nobody ever said because everybody knew.

She wondered if that included Liam. Rooting in her bag for her keyring, she wondered if that had been the reason he'd spent so much time doing dope.

Here were her keys. She used them, stepped inside, and felt resistance as she pushed the door closed behind her, the sudden bulk of a body blocking her, and

panic

it was amazing how swiftly it descended, dropped like a net. It was what the city trained you for. All that crazy pavement stuff happened in public, but anywhere you were alone, the possibility of contact increased. Both kinds of contact, good and bad.

Mostly bad.

"*Get off me!*"

She was inside Lunchbox, her everyday destination, and someone had come in with her. His big hands were guiding her in, keeping her facing forwards, while he kicked the door shut behind them. The grey morning light was replaced by its green-tinted replica. The floor was a big shiny rink.

There was nobody here. She was always first.

"*Get off—*"

"Flea."

Released, she jumped forward, out of the reach of the intruder's grasp. The nearest phone was on the nearest desk—no, the nearest phone was in her bag, but if she got tangled up trying to retrieve it, he might—

"Flea."

She reached the desk, grabbed the phone, and yelped as an alien hand slammed it back down. He'd moved so fast, was right with her still—

"Flea," Bettany said again. "It's me."

And barely flinched at all when she slapped his face as hard as she could.

"You mad bastard!"

She swung at him again, a blow easily avoided.

He caught her by the wrist.

"You want to stop this now."

"*Stop* this? *Stop* this?"

For some reason his instruction snagged on her mind.

"You want me to *stop* this?"

He released her and she swung again immediately, both hands this time. She wanted to claw his eyes out. She'd been *kind* to him, this mad bastard, she'd been *kind* to him when Liam died, and look how he'd repaid her.

And then he had her wrist again and this time he spun her round so he was spooning her upright, and his free hand clamped across her mouth just as she was about to scream.

It was as easy as this, she thought. Middle of the city. You could be murdered as easily as this, and the world would keep spinning, and no one would come to your rescue.

"I really need you to be quiet," he said.

Her heart was going to burst.

He removed his hand.

"I'm not here to hurt you."

"Then why—you *frightened* me—"

And hadn't stopped frightening her, in fact, because she could feel something pressing against her, something in his coat pocket, something hard and metal and unforgiving.

"Is that—?"

He released her, and she half-stepped half-staggered away from him and came to a bump against a desk.

"What's that in your pocket?"

"There's something I need you to do."

"Is that a *gun*?"

"Flea? Your colleagues. When do they usually get here?"

"You came here with a *gun*?"

"I need you to make sure they don't come in. Are you listening?"

Flea ran.

4.4

Earlier that morning, Boo Berryman had been for a jog—the sky dark and the air damp. The tube ran overland near Vincent's house, and one rattled past as Boo entered the narrow lane to the common. It held few passengers. From Boo's perspective they looked frozen in place, a tableau of raincoat, misted window and conversation-proof newspaper.

He rounded the common counterclockwise three times. Dog-walkers made tracks here and there, their charges snuffling busily in their wake, and a few other joggers overtook him as he ran. Boo wasn't built for speed, but the early shift appealed to him. The air tasted different then.

The slapping of feet on wet grass. The barking of dogs. Another train rattled past, heading the other way. Even emptier, that direction.

A lot of joggers listened to their iPods as they ran. Others used the time "to think." For Boo it was a clearing out. For however long it took him he was simply a body on the move, a machine going through its paces. His brain registered the physical effort he was making, and dimly catalogued surroundings, and that was all.

Circuits done, Boo slowed to a walk. His knee was protesting, and he knew better than to force it into submission. Back at the lane he did his stretches before heading for the pavement, and falling back into the day.

Bishop must have dozed off in his chair because he definitely came round from something, a sensation of weight being let slip. His hands were empty. He blinked, worked out where he was, and reached for his phone.

"Yeah, it's me again. Okay, listen, that barman reckons he saw Boyd? Says he was carrying his son's ashes in a bag. Yeah, I know. So maybe it's crazy, but what if it isn't? Maybe Boyd was out on the streets same night he saw his kid burned, maybe that's what sent him mad enough to show his face again . . . Yeah. So first thing, or make that now, get some bodies round the local crems, crematoria, see who they had on their books Tuesday . . . What? It's the plural. It is. Look, just get it done. We're looking for someone the right age to be Boyd's son, so anyone up to, I don't know, mid-twenties. No, not called Boyd. Anything but Boyd . . . Okay. And make it fast."

The letting slip sensation, Bishop had been dreaming he'd been carrying that bag himself. One of the gifts the sleeping world bequeaths to the waking. And that was another thought that drifted away like smoke as he gathered his daytime self around him, and wondered whether it was too soon to let the Brothers McGarry know it was happening at last, their revenge taking shape.

But no. Leave it be for now, he decided.

Wait until they had the actual Martin Boyd nailed down tight, no disappointments. After that, well, everybody's day could only get better.

Guest of honour excepted, of course.

Boo didn't yet know Vincent's plans, but hoped he'd opt for the office. It wasn't good for Vincent to go hermit. Boo thought of it like wandering into a forest. Vincent liked it because it was peaceful and shady and he could hear himself think, but there was always the danger that if he wandered too far, he'd not find his way back.

Boo's job, as he'd always understood it, was to make sure that never happened.

He let himself into the kitchen, scooping a towel from the back of a chair, throwing it round his neck. There was a warmth in the air. Putting a palm to the kettle, he could tell it had recently boiled. An early morning, which meant Vincent was planning to head into Lunchbox. Boo's spirits lightened.

Maybe today would be a good day.

The next time Marten Saar showed his face, the sun had made inroads on the day. His renewed acquaintance with the girls in his bedroom had left him a little less restless, a little more relaxed, and altogether readier to face the view from his window, which was more clearly delineated now. Harsh lines kept the buildings separate, the traffic had rediscovered primary colours, and if the ghosts on the pavement were still ant-sized, there were more of them. He lit a cigarette, an action performed so fluently it might not have occurred to him he was doing so.

He was thinking about the Cousins' Circle again.

At some point during the last couple of hours, when to all obvious intent his mind, like the rest of him, was occupied with anything but business, he'd arrived at a decision. Which was that he'd agree to Oskar's strategy. The lean years were behind them at last, and the current success would mean nothing if they didn't build. This twenty-second floor had been hard-won, but it was an eyrie, not an empire, and if the next step required dangerous alliance, so be it. That was how wars were won. He could all but hear those words rasping from his friend's tobacco-mangled throat. And there was no shame in a general taking advice from a street-fighter. Oskar was wily. He'd run rings round the local Blues last year, when they'd held him for shooting a hard-case. If Marten was going to make cause with the Cousins he wanted Oskar beside him, ensuring these new friends stayed honest.

Two more good years. Three. Then he'd swap this shit-hole in the sky for someplace more solid, where he could feel London's rumblings through his boots.

Rumblings there were up here too, but just the usual ones. Noises from bedrooms, from the plasma screen, from the kitchen, the usual guttural rumblings of men feeding and buffing them-selves and lazing about, waiting for instructions or the promise of action. No knowing how they'd take the thought of allying themselves with another crew, especially a bigger one, stronger and more Russian. Except that it didn't matter how they'd take the thought, all that mattered was they do the deed. Take their orders, carry them out. Nobody had to be told that their lock on the market wouldn't last forever. Adapt and thrive. It wasn't just market sense, it was evolution.

Oskar would appreciate that, Marten decided, but calling his name got no response. He asked where he'd got to, but drew a blank. Oskar had gone out. Nobody knew where.

It didn't please Marten. What was the point of a right hand

if it detached itself at will? But he'd be back, and arrangements would be made, and next steps taken, alliances forged.

Meanwhile, he'd go shower.

There was only one candidate. Nice, the way things sometimes turned out. The only body fed to the flames in N1 Tuesday last who wasn't old, female or black was one Liam Bettany, whose address Bishop now had.

Clickety-click, he thought. The sound you got if you listened carefully to a lock being turned, the tumblers falling. *Clickety-click.* Someone released, someone shut in.

The kid had died in a fall from a window, high on dope. Put that together with Boyd, who was maybe called Bettany, going looking for dealers, making use of old contacts to get a gun, and what you had was your basic revenge scenario.

Once you knew what someone was doing, the second-guess became possible.

Muskrat came from a single source, an Estonian crew headed by Marten Saar, who'd been a gutter rat for decades but was lately thinking big. His next-man-down was Oskar Kask, and Bishop had had dealings with him. He was a short man, lazy-looking eyes, but it would be an idea not to be taken in by either because his height didn't matter and his laziness was a mask. Bishop recognised the signs. A repressed electric charge throbbed off Oskar Kask, as if he were looking for an excuse to do you harm. If Boyd/Bettany was planning on taking on that crew, it was really only Kask he had to worry about.

But that was a worry he'd be saved from. There'd be no joy for the Brothers McGarry if Boyd wound up stuffed in someone else's dustbin. They wanted something to take the chill off the long locked-in evenings, which meant a few farewell words of apology and terror, followed by drawn-out suffering. Something they could replay over and over, without getting tired of.

Clickety-click. It was only fourteen hours since Martin Boyd had picked up the gun, and he'd hardly expect them to be this close already. But the kind of luck he'd been living on couldn't last forever. Even he must know that. Or soon would.

4.5

Bettany caught her by the stairs, his hand round her elbow. He pushed her against the wall.

"Flea. Listen."

"You're here to kill him!"

"I don't want to hurt anyone."

"Then why have you got a *gun*?"

She was shouting. This was no good. This wasn't the calm exchange of information he'd been hoping for.

"Flea—"

"Don't *touch* me."

He had to know when others would start turning up. Had to make sure they didn't.

"Look—"

There was a loud banging on glass.

The pair froze, as if both were guilty.

The letterbox rattled, and someone called through it.

"Flea? That you? Let us in, will ya?"

"Haydn," whispered Flea.

"Can he—"

"No. Not through the tinted glass."

"I know you're there. Stop messing around."

"He's always forgetting his key," she whispered.

"Get rid of him."

"Why don't you just shoot him?"

"I'm not here to shoot anyone. Look, just trust me, okay?"

"*Trust* you?"

"Flea! The door?"

"I don't even know you. You turned up out of nowhere with a beard. Now it's like you're someone else. And I don't know either of you!"

Bettany took half a moment to work his way through that one.

"Just get rid of him, can you do that? I'm not here to hurt anyone, but we really don't need company."

"And what if I just run? What if I open the door for him and leg it down the street? Will you follow? With your *gun*?"

"No," he said. "I won't."

The look on her face suggested she'd been expecting a threat.

"You were Liam's friend," he said. "Can you be mine too?"

"Flea! Open the bloody door, woman!"

She said, "If you're lying . . ."

But there was nowhere for that sentence to go.

He stood by the stairs while she went to the front door and opened it a notch. He couldn't hear precisely what she said, but it included the words *Vincent*, *home* and *today*.

It was effective enough. A moment later she was closing the door, walking back.

He said, "The others. They'll start arriving soon, right?"

"What do you want me to do about it?"

Challenging now, as if she'd weighed up the whole matter of the gun he was carrying, and decided it wasn't all that.

"Call them," he said. "Put them off."

"I'm not going to help you hurt Vincent."

"I don't want you to. I just want you to keep your colleagues out of the way."

"Because you think he had something to do with Liam's death."

"And what if he did?"

"He didn't."

"But what if—"

"He *didn't*."

It wasn't clear which of them was most taken aback by her vehemence.

He said, "I just need to ask him a few questions."

"You already did that."

"This time he'll answer them."

"Because you've got a gun."

"I'm not going to hurt him, Flea. I promise."

She shook her head.

"Will you call them?"

Flea stared at him long and hard, apparently believing this would impress upon him the serious consequences that might yet befall him. It made him want to smile. Before he could succumb to the temptation, she produced her mobile and began the process of telling her colleagues not to come in today.

Bettany paced, walked off his adrenalin spike. He'd had no sleep—when you were making enemies, even small ones like JK Coe, lazy ones like Dancer Blaine, you didn't rest your head in the usual places. Not until you were ready for them to find you.

The light was aquarium green. He scooped the softball off the floor, lofted it at the waiting net. It spun on the rim for a second, then dropped back.

Liam had worked here. How many times had he played with this ball, that net? Was he a good shot? Had practice made him expert?

He shook his head. The reasons you had, the ones that kept you going, you didn't need them at the forefront of your mind. They'd muddle your vision. As long as the job lasted, you had to keep them warm and hidden. Only then could you take them out, check they hadn't spoiled in the darkness.

Thoughts of Liam had to wait. They shouldn't take up head-room now.

He'd spent the early hours by the canal, walking the towpath, slumping on the occasional bench while frost formed on stones. There'd been others out there but nobody approached him, with fair motive or foul. That had been just as well.

He wasn't tired, that was the odd thing. It was as if all the daily weaknesses had melted away, returning him to the state he'd known in one of his previous lives. He was becoming Martin Boyd again. Who'd known how to get a job done.

Ask the Brothers McGarry.

Flea finished on the phone.

"What time will Vincent get here?" he asked.

She shrugged. "An hour?"

An hour.

"Let's get some coffee," he said.

4.6

It was more like eighty minutes. They spent the first thirty mostly in silence, until Bettany realised Flea was staring at him unwaveringly—rarely blinking. She might have been studying a new kind of frog.

As much to break her spell as anything, he said, "What Liam told you. About what I used to do."

"He said you were a spy."

"It's true. I worked for the Intelligence Services."

"But not any more."

"Not any more, no."

"And what happened to Liam—it didn't have anything to do with that, did it?"

Bettany didn't reply.

"You think it did?"

He said, "What does Driscoll do?"

"Vincent? You know what he does. He designs games."

"Is that all?"

She shook her head, but not in answer to his question. More at the absurdity of it.

"Don't tell me. You think game writing's his cover? What, you think he's working on some, some, some kind of mind control thing? Or designing a super-duper virus that'll—"

"He works in cyber-systems, and that's—"

"—I don't know, knock out enemy weapon systems? Who are our enemies these days, anyway?"

"—always of interest to the Service."

"The Service," she said.

"The Intelligence Service."

"I know what you meant. It's the way you said it. As if it was the Church or something. Church with a capital."

He said, "It was a job, that's all. But one that cast a long shadow. I thought I'd left it behind, but it seems to have caught me up. Caught Liam up."

"You really think that, don't you? That Liam's dead because of what you used to be?"

"I don't believe in coincidence."

"It isn't a coincidence. Liam dying isn't a *coincidence*. If you'd been a, a, a doctor, would his death have anything to do with that?"

Instead of answering, Bettany stood. Reflections from the canal drew shimmery nothings across the ceiling. He walked towards the windows.

"What's the matter?"

"You were a friend to Liam," he said. "Thank you for that."

She didn't reply.

"We need to be upstairs now."

Eventually, Vincent arrived.

He came through the street-side door, and because no one else had used that door this morning had to open it with a key. This cast a puzzled air over his footsteps, which they heard reach the centre of the office before he called out.

"Where is everyone?"

He wasn't used to raising his voice, Bettany could tell. It had probably been a while since he'd had cause to. When you were rich, people made the effort to listen.

Flea called, "We're up here, Vincent."

"Flea?"

"Up here."

"Where is everyone?"

But he was coming up the stairs.

"Flea?"

He was in the office before he realised they weren't alone.

"Mr. Bettany?"

"You on your own?"

"What are you doing here? Where's everyone else?"

"Are you alone?"

"It's all right, Vincent, it's just—"

"Quiet. Driscoll. Are you on your own?"

"Boo's just parking. Flea, what is this? Did you let him in? And—"

"She didn't let me in, Driscoll. I turned up."

The front door opened again and Boo Berryman came in. They heard his footsteps reach the centre of the hallway, then stop.

"Better get him up here," Bettany said.

"Boo?" Vincent called. "We're up here. With Mr. Bettany."

Boo was quiet on the stairs, and entered the office carefully, trying to take everything in at once. "You okay?" he asked.

His question was for the others, but his eyes were on Bettany.

"You might want to stand over there," Bettany said, indicating the wall to his left.

Boo Berryman said, "Is this a joke? You want me to get rid of him?"

Bettany glanced window-wards, then pulled the Makarov from his pocket.

"You said you wouldn't—" began Flea.

"Quiet. You two. Against the wall."

He meant Boo and the girl. Driscoll, he wanted to stay where he was, just this side of the desk.

Boo said, "You piece of shit."

"Yeah yeah. Against the wall."

"I should take that off you and—"

"Boo," Driscoll said. "Let's do as he says."

Driscoll seemed the calmest, thought Bettany. Well, that figured. He gave the impression of being sealed behind glass.

See how long that lasts.

Boo and Flea stood in front of the movie poster. Bettany kicked the door shut and pointed the gun at Driscoll, waggling it briefly towards the opposite wall.

"You want me to move."

"That's the general idea."

Driscoll did, leaving Bettany with a clear view through the window behind the desk.

"What are you after, Mr Bettany?"

"Answers."

"I can assure you, nobody here had anything to do with your son's death."

"Have I asked any questions yet?"

"...No."

"Then shut up."

Bettany glanced at Flea briefly and lowered the gun. Then looked at Boo.

"Don't get clever. Even if both knees worked, you'd not get near me."

Boo sneered.

"So what are your questions, Mr. Bettany?" Driscoll asked.

Bettany noted the *mister*. Grace under pressure, he thought. Then again, Driscoll might be taking the piss.

He said, "Why aren't you getting richer off your new game?" and was rewarded with a dumbfounded look.

There, he thought. That got a response.

The landlord wore a corduroy shirt and was called Greenleaf. Good name, thought Bishop. He looked like a strong gust would tear him off and blow him away.

Bishop said, "You've got an upstairs flat, one a kid took a dive from?"

"It was an accident."

"I'm sure. Anyone there at the moment?"

"There's a temporary occupant."

"He around?"

Greenleaf sneered. "Says he's the father. Says what's left of the tenancy's his by rights. I should have consulted my solicitor. He could be anyone, know what I'm saying?"

"But he's not here now?"

"Turned up with a beard, looking like he crawled from under a bridge."

"Tidied himself up, did he?"

"Still smells a wrong 'un."

But either way, he wasn't in.

Greenleaf didn't want to part with a key, but maybe Bishop like smelled a wrong 'un too, because it only took a hard stare to change his mind. He retreated with a grumbled litany of a type familiar to Bishop, one that would increase in bravery once doors were closed, and Bishop elsewhere. This didn't faze Bishop. Indeed, its absence would cause him worry.

He was quiet entering the flat, for all its vacancy. Always assume there's a sleeping dog. There wasn't, but he stuck his head into every room before marginally relaxing, and saw nothing bar junkie-bait—laptop, iPod, TV. Not what he was here for.

Which was an indication Bettany would be back. Greenleaf reckoned he was roosting, but Bettany was a pro. All he needed was a plan—or failing that, an opportunity—and he'd put his vengeance into motion. After that, the last place he'd been was the last place he'd come back to. His son's flat would gather dust until the rent ran out.

So Bishop turned the place over, opening drawers, checking behind radiators. He found a baggie of muskrat, definitely the son's—pros don't get stoned, not on enemy territory. Bedroom and bathroom done, he returned to the kitchen. Nothing in the fridge, nothing in the oven—single men, living alone, the oven was often a good place to hide things. There, or under a pile of takeaway cartons. But everything was neat and clean, the dope the only hint of dissipation. A little touch of oblivion the kid wouldn't be needing now.

Bettany had been sleeping on the couch. A cushion bore the imprint of his head.

But there was nothing to indicate that he was coming back, or nothing until Bishop finally took note of what was staring him in the face. Not hidden—that was the trick of it—but out in the open, on the kitchen table.

You are kidding, he thought.

But he wasn't, or it wasn't. This was it, the famous bag, a cloth one with a book cover on it, *Brighton Rock*. Soft, unstructured, it had collapsed around its contents, taking on the shape of the urn which Bishop lifted out now. Smaller than you'd expect, even to Bishop, who'd seen bodies crammed into pretty tiny places. He unscrewed the lid and dipped a finger in. Dust and grit and what looked like plaque, the stuff you spat into a basin when the dentist scraped your teeth.

Bishop had to resist the impulse to lick his finger clean.

He screwed the lid on and replaced the tin in the bag. Checked to make sure he'd left nothing out of place, then went downstairs.

"You won't be mentioning this to Mr. Bettany."

Some you had to bribe, and some you simply had to inform.

Greenleaf said, "I checked the rent book. He's only got till Wednesday."

If he's lucky, thought Bishop.

"I'll hang onto the key for the moment," he said. "If that's all right with you."

It wasn't a question.

Back at the car he made a few calls. Half an hour from now the area would be covered, every junction with its own pair of eyes, its own pair of hands.

Bettany was coming back. Didn't matter where he was right now, he'd have to come back for his son. No way would he leave him on the kitchen table. One minute after the rent was due, that goblin of a landlord would rinse the urn and put it on eBay.

He cracked his knuckles. Funny, he thought. He was thinking of him as Bettany now. For years he'd been Martin Boyd, even though for seven of those years everyone knew he'd been no one of the sort, but now he had the name Bettany, and it fitted him like a glove.

Just one of the things that would be peeled from him before long.

A car arrived, four occupants, all familiar. Bishop pointed to the flat, then gave two fingers each to both ends of the road. A nod from the driver and off the car went. A white van followed it, its windowless back doors coated in muck. I WISH MY OLD LADY WAS AS DIRTY AS THIS someone had scrawled. You ever saw a clean white van, first thing you'd do was alert the police. *It was obviously suspicious, officer. Someone had washed it.*

No knowing how long this would take, but there wasn't a desperate hurry. Think of the Brothers McGarry—they had nothing but time, thanks to Bettany. There was three years of his own life he'd not be getting back too. That kind of thing taught you patience.

4.7

Through the window something distantly flashed—a faraway jet, a dab of moisture on an aerial, a shard of glass in a magpie's beak. Anything or nothing. Some reflections produce themselves.

"It's not really a new game," Driscoll said. "Just a new generation of the old one. But yes, you're right, I'm not going to be making money off it."

"Why not?"

"Because I'm giving it away."

For some reason it felt like just the two of them now. Bettany knew Boo Berryman was weighing him up, drawing mental diagrams showing arrows and tipping points and the loose trajectories of unintentional bullets, but he also knew that any move Boo Berryman made, he might as well send Flea Pointer in front waving a red flag. Boo thought he was match-fit, but he didn't worry Bettany.

He said, "Is that usual?"

"Is that your second question?"

"Call it a follow-up."

Driscoll gave the slightest of nods, as if this were a perfectly reasonable request in a perfectly reasonable conversation.

"It happens. Lots of companies release free product."

"Usually because they plan to make money off it some other way. Which you don't, apparently."

Driscoll retreated inside himself a little way, then came back. He removed his glasses. Without their tinted lenses, his face seemed paler.

He said, "Okay, if it means so much to you. And because you're holding a gun. I'm giving it away because it's old news. *Shades* made money because it was a good idea. It appealed to the conspiracy theorist inside every gamer. They all think there's something being kept from us, so giving them a game which played on this was bound to be a winner. So the second one was bound to be a winner too, because the same people were always going to buy it, even if they didn't like it as much. Gamers are completists. But a third . . . I wrote *Shades 3*, Mr. Bettany, because I couldn't find a way not to. Because I hate to leave a story unfinished. But I'm giving it away because it'll never make money anyway. Its moment has passed."

"So what are your marketing people for? Window dressing?"

Disconcertingly, Driscoll laughed.

"I supposed they are, really. All of this . . ."

He indicated the building they stood in.

"It makes for a good show. And the team, they do their best. They're very . . . *involved*. Except it turns out that playing games is easier than inventing them."

"But not for you."

Driscoll said, "I got lucky. Why did you want to know all that?"

"Because I've asked before. And nobody answered."

"You must live life in a very straight line."

"I'm not the only one. I presume the reason nobody answered is you're keeping it quiet for now. Why's that?"

"Another follow-up?"

"Mmm-hm."

Driscoll said, "It's not going to be popular with the shareholders."

"I'll bet."

"Not that they can stop me. I own fifty-five per cent of the company. But I'm not sure it's entirely secret. There's been a bit of gossip."

He didn't look Flea's way saying this, but Bettany suspected that took effort.

Driscoll said, "So what was your second question?"

"What?"

"You said you had two questions. What was the second?"

"Oh, right," said Bettany. "Second question. What happens when I do this?"

Pointing the gun towards Driscoll, he pulled the trigger.

Dame Ingrid was on walkabout.

She'd circled the hub, Ops territory, and bearded Diana Taverner in her den—Taverner Second-Desked Ops, and could turn a 360 loop without ever taking her eyes off Dame Ingrid's job. Dropping in unexpectedly, which Tearney did every third or fourth time the thought occurred to her (it was important to keep these events random), was a way of reminding Lady Di whose shadow she walked in. After that she'd been touring the hallways, buttonholing the odd virgin (*"And what is it you do?"*, the monarchical phrasing only partly satirical) and generally playing up to the image, when the mobile in her pocket whined like an incoming doodlebug.

CALL ME the text read. Since when was she issued instructions?

There was a slight fraying on her right cuff. Since then, maybe. Since cuffs started to fray.

She took the lift further down, below the streets, below the daylight.

More than half of London was underground. Another city shadowing the first. A lot of what happened in this secret city quite rightly took place out of sight of the sun, from little sins in the subways to the sometimes quite frightening events triggered in the vast network of corridors and rooms beneath Whitehall. And here under Regent's Park, some floors below the one at which she alighted now, various events had occurred in recent years which it was occasionally her duty to deny had ever taken place. *Not on English soil* was her preferred phrase. Such things— the treatment of suspects, the over-rigorous pursuit of testimony—*did not take place on English soil*, as she had stated more than once to more than one committee. And this remained the legal truth of the matter, as the things in question were taking place some distance below that.

No matter now. Instead, the level at which she emerged housed Strategy, sometimes called the Zoo, because strategy wonks were frequently nocturnal, often unsocialised, and usually in need of a shower. But for obvious reasons, they also had the most secure offices.

"I need to make a call," she informed the really quite attractive young man with a Security laminate who was posted by the lifts.

"Of course, Dame Ingrid."

He led her along the corridor to an empty room which buzzed a little, a white-static fizz that acted like a mosquito net, though it sounded like a mosquito. It was an audible security blanket, indicating that the room was unbugged, unbuggable.

She thanked him, said that was all, and he left.

There was a white phone—rotary dial—on an otherwise bare table, desk height, and she picked this up and rang a number from memory.

"It's me."

"He's made his move."

"Good."

"Not entirely."

She said, "Choose your words carefully."

"Plan A didn't happen."

She thought about this, and the voice down the line went quiet while she did so.

Thinking about it, though, wasn't going to get anyone far. There'd only ever been two plans, A and B. A had been for Tom Bettany to put a bullet in Vincent Driscoll's head. B was messier, but would get the job done.

"All right," she said. "You know what to do."

He hung up without replying, as she'd known he would. He wasn't a joe but he had a joe's bones, using few words and leaving few traces. And knew there was no point discussing what was, when you came down to it, an order.

She recradled the receiver, a small part of her brain enjoying the old-fashionedness of the action, once an everyday occurrence, but increasingly retro. Mostly, though, she was shuffling cards in her head. Plan B was now plan A. Proceed accordingly, she told herself. Wiping all trace of plan A from her mind, she left the room to find the really quite attractive young man with a Security laminate waiting.

Behind her, the room carried on quietly buzzing.

4.8

The shot set the lightbulbs humming.

Boo Berryman, give him credit, leaped forward. If he'd rung a bell first, he couldn't have given more warning. Stepping aside, Bettany cracked his head with the gun as he passed. Boo hit the floor with a thud that shook more plaster from the fresh hole in the wall.

Flea's short sharp cry added a higher pitch to the mix.

Ignoring Bettany, Vincent Driscoll stepped forward and knelt by Boo's side.

"Did you have to do that?"

"Instinct," said Bettany.

Partly true, but he didn't like being jumped at.

The noises shivered away.

Berryman groaned.

"I don't know what to do," Vincent said.

He was looking at Flea.

"There's a first aid kit downstairs."

"He'll be okay," Bettany said. "It was only a tap."

A further groan from Boo suggested a second opinion.

"Make him sit up."

Vincent struggled with the recumbent Boo, and Flea came forward to help.

Bettany stepped aside, looking towards the window again. Whatever had flashed earlier wasn't flashing now. Either it or the sun had moved.

"Why did you shoot?"

"Mmm?"

"For God's sake . . . You could have killed someone."

"I wanted to know what would happen."

He was distracted, focused on what was—or wasn't—going on through the window. Then he snapped back to himself.

"Sit him up against the wall."

"He's bleeding."

"It's just a scrape. He'll be fine."

"I think he's concussed."

"He'll be fine."

Vincent rose. For the first time in Bettany's experience, he seemed totally present. He said, "What just happened?"

"I pointed a gun at you. Fired it. In full view of that window."

"And what did that tell you?"

"That someone wants you dead," said Bettany.

Vincent wore much the expression he adopted when faced with a programming problem. It spoke of enjoyable puzzlement.

"How does firing a gun at me prove that?"

"It tells me that nobody's looking out for you."

From the floor, Boo Berryman groaned.

"Okay, Tarzan did his best. But I was warned off you by some serious people, and they knew the warning didn't take.

If it had, I'd be long gone." He paused. "London isn't a healthy place for me."

"He's a spy," Flea said.

"Used to be. But the point is, if my former employers really wanted to keep you safe, they'd have someone watching your back. And the moment I raised a gun in full view of that window, I'd have been dead."

Vincent looked towards the window, as if it offered proof of this assertion. But the proof was a negative. There were clear angles of sight through the windows to the rooftops opposite, where no marksmen waited, keeping an eye on Vincent Driscoll.

"There was someone there," Bettany said. "On a rooftop, other side of the canal. They're gone now. But they were watching to see what happened. And the fact that they didn't try to stop me means they wanted me to do it."

"Shoot me."

Bettany nodded.

Flea said, "Warned you off how?"

Bettany's reply was directed at Vincent. "I was told you had nothing to do with Liam's death. Which meant one of two things."

From the floor, Boo Berryman spoke. "That he had nothing to do with Liam's death," he said. "Or else he had everything to do with it."

"Told you he'd be okay," Bettany said.

"Bastard," Boo said.

He was slurring, but not badly. The graze on his temple looked nasty though, a rough red slice of skin.

Vincent said, "Someone told you I was innocent to make you think the opposite?"

"Like pinning a target on your back."

"So someone set me up."

"Set us both up. Me to kill you. You to be dead."

"Why?"

"There's a question. Who've you upset lately?"

Vincent said, "I don't go round upsetting people."

"Really? What about your shareholders?"

Flea said, "Oh, God."

"Brand new product, long-awaited by all your fans. Part three in a successful series. And you're planning on giving it away like something in a cereal box."

Bettany put the gun back in his pocket.

He said, "You can see how that might make some people tetchy."

"I've explained that. It's not like—"

"You're missing the point. What happens if you die?"

Vincent said, "I've not really given it any thought."

Still sitting, Boo said, "He means to the company. To Lunch-box."

"My shares will be sold. Current shareholders get preferential rates . . ."

"And plans will change," said Bettany. "Specifically, the one involving giving your product away."

"Oh . . ."

"Yeah. Oh. You might want to give that some thought." He turned to leave.

Flea said, "Hey!"

"What?"

"You can't just go!"

He hesitated. "Do you trust me?"

"What?"

"Do you trust me?"

"... I don't know."

"Well do," he said, and left.

Boo said, "Could someone get me a glass of water?"

Bettany's footsteps had faded away.

"Please?"

"I'll go," Flea said.

She headed off down to the kitchen area.

Once she'd gone, Boo said, "Vincent?"

"It's coming. She's gone for some water."

"He's right, you know," Boo said.

"About what?"

"You're in danger. Somebody wants you dead because you're planning on giving away a fortune."

Vincent said, "There's not going to be a fortune."

"Yeah, but—"

"It'd sell a few thousand copies at best. To completists. The thing is, Boo, it's really not very good."

"Will you shut up a second?"

Vincent frowned.

Boo heaved himself upright, and rubbed the ugly mark on his temple. Then he shook his head, as if having trouble focusing. He said, "God, that's gonna hurt tomorrow. Hurts today, if you want to know the truth."

"There's a first aid kit somewhere. Flea will find it."

Boo gripped Vincent's elbow.

"Listen to me. It doesn't matter what *Shades 3*'s like, it's still going to make somebody a fortune if they can stop you giving it away. If you die, that plan's buried with you. And let's face it, you being dead'll make pretty good publicity."

Vincent said, "Could you let go of my elbow please?"

"Sorry."

"I know you're looking out for me. I'm just finding all this a little hard to believe."

"That guy shot at you. Here. In your office. And you're still having trouble believing something's up?"

"His son died. He's upset."

"So am I. He hit me, you probably noticed. But he's not the one we need to be worrying about, Vincent. He's not the one who wants you dead."

Then Boo paused.

He said, "Did you hear that?"

4.9

Oskar Kask entered through the towpath door, having crossed the canal by the arching brick bridge. The rooftop from which he'd been watching events inside Lunchbox was the garden of an apartment block, not two hundred yards distant, and he suspected Bettany had seen him there, or seen something. A sunflash off his binoculars, his own sudden movement. He hadn't told Dame Spook this. She would have wondered whether it had skewed the result, becoming the reason why Bettany buried the bullet in the wall instead of in Driscoll's head.

The door to the building opened with a hiss. The floor was clean, hard, tiled. He crossed it making little noise, but not caring unduly if he did. Speed mattered more than stealth.

Upstairs, the talking stopped.

Halfway up to the first landing, he produced an automatic from a shoulder holster, and began screwing a silencer onto its barrel.

"It was Flea."

"Flea didn't go out," Boo said. "That was the front door."

He was on his feet, putting a hand to his head. His palm came away moist.

"Call the police," he said.

"What are you doing?"

"Call the police. And lock the door. Does this door lock? Lock it."

"Boo—"

But Boo was already lumbering from the office. The jarring motion as he pulled the door shut set his head ringing. Damn Bettany for clubbing him when he needed to be sharp.

A man was coming up the stairs, a short man with frizzy hair and a heavy blue chin. He held a gun in one hand.

Boo's morning kaleidoscoped, and trains rattled past. The slapping of feet on wet grass and the barking of dogs. The warmth of the kettle against his palm. His knee gave a twinge, and his head was abuzz, and he'd spent the past six years half-expecting a moment like this one, and here it was. If he didn't feel ready, that was just how life worked. You were never ready for the really bad moments.

The man levelled his gun at Boo as he crested the stairs, moving swiftly towards him.

Then Tom Bettany stepped out of Flea Pointer's office and pressed the barrel of his own gun to the man's temple.

"Drop it."

The man stopped, dropped his gun and raised his hands, without—it seemed to Boo—altering the blank expression on his face.

Bettany kicked the gun away.

Boo said, "So you came back."

"I never left. Ever seen him before?"

Boo shook his head, then realised Bettany wasn't watching him. His eyes were fixed on the newcomer. He said, "No. Never."

"Well, take a good look now. He came here to kill your boss."

"You know who he is?"

"I know he likes to hang around crematoriums. You bring your thermos with you?"

The man's lip twitched, but he said nothing.

"What's going on? Who's he?"

It was Flea, coming up the stairs behind them, a glass of water in one hand and a plastic first-aid satchel in the other.

"Tom?"

"He came back," Boo said.

Flea stopped on the staircase. She could only see the back of the newcomer's head, but the gun on the floor told half the story, and Bettany's gun told the other.

"You knew he was coming."

"I warned you."

"No, you *knew*."

She put the first-aid kit on the stair in front of her.

Bettany said, "I told you Driscoll was in danger."

"You didn't tell us he was *bait*."

"He's still alive, isn't he?"

As if to settle this matter, Vincent stepped into the hallway. He said, "I couldn't call the police. My phone's in the car."

Bettany glanced towards him, and the gunman made his move.

PART FIVE

5.1

He was half a second off his game. Maybe less.

Enough of a gap for the gunman to slip through.

Bettany had glanced away and the stranger had been waiting. He didn't go for his weapon, which was smart, because that was on the floor behind Bettany.

He went for Flea Pointer instead.

Who screamed.

Bettany levelled his gun at the man's head but couldn't get a clean sight, because the man had an arm round Flea's neck, and had swung her in front of him.

"Let her go."

That was Driscoll.

Bettany didn't speak. He moved sideways, arms outstretched, gun level. The man retreated in synch, Flea's heels dragging on the floor.

"Let her *go!*"

"Shut. Up," Bettany said.

Flea's eyes were wide as doorways, and she was gripping the man's arm with both hands but couldn't speak. A gurgling noise was all she could manage.

Bettany changed sides and still the man moved with him, edging back towards the stairs, half his head shielded by Flea's.

There was a yard between them, if that. A yard and Flea Pointer, whose face was scarlet.

Now Berryman spoke.

"We can take him."

Flea's frantic look suggested otherwise.

"Stay back," Bettany said without turning.

"He won't hurt her. He won't dare."

"Stay. Back."

It was noise. The two men behind him, Flea herself, were noise. Only the signal mattered. The signal was the gunman. It was what his eyes broadcast. That was where Bettany would read the future, or the next little fragment of it.

And the signal passed both ways, because every move he made, the other echoed.

They'd slow-waltzed to the top of the staircase. Without looking behind, the gunman sensed this and halted.

His hair was a grey frizz, his eyes dark. Like a rubber ball, he radiated the impression of stored kinetic energy.

Had he killed Liam?

Bettany pushed the thought away. The man was Ingrid Tearney's tool, that was clear, but all that mattered now was whether he'd hurt Flea Pointer before Bettany could take him down.

He said, "Let her go."

No reply.

"You can't make it down the stairs. Not without releasing her. Let her go."

There was movement behind him and Bettany cursed inwardly but didn't turn.

The man said, "I could break her neck."

Was that an American accent? But he might be disguising his voice, or parroting English learned at his television's knee.

Bettany said, "And you'll be dead the next second."

"You don't want to kill me."

Boo Berryman said, "Maybe I do. Let her go."

He'd picked up the discarded gun and held it the same way Bettany held his, right hand clasped around the handle, left hand steadying his wrist, with the crucial difference that the idiot didn't know what he was doing.

A brief smile tickled the lip of the gunman.

Bettany said, "Put that down. Get back in the office. Leave this to me."

"This is my job."

"It's not a job, you moron—"

And there was the second gap.

Bettany'd barely flicked his eyes Boo's way but it was enough, because Flea Pointer was crashing into him and he only just had time to raise the gun, point it ceilingwards in case the contact caused him to pull the trigger. It didn't, but the impact of Flea's body knocked him down anyway—

"Stop!"

That was Boo, standing at the top of the stairs, pointing the gun at the fleeing stranger's back.

"Stop!"

But he didn't. He took the stairs a flight at a time, leaping down to each landing like an Olympian in a hurry.

Bettany tried to get up, but Flea was clinging to him.

"Couldn't ... breathe ..."

"I need to get after him—"

"Here."

Vincent Driscoll prised her loose.

She went to him readily, wrapping her arms round him while she sobbed and gasped for air.

Bettany scrabbled to his feet and took off.

Boo Berryman was left standing, the gun he'd snatched hanging heavy at his side. He said "Stop" again, but mostly to himself, and nobody noticed.

Two drops of water raced each other down the window pane, enjoying random bursts of speed they then frittered away on unnecessary diversions. Before either reached the sill, JK Coe lost patience with them. He wanted to raise a hand and smash the glass. That he didn't spoke more of torpor than restraint.

He was in his kitchen. Coming on lunchtime, but he wasn't hungry. If he ate he'd throw up everywhere, and that would be another room closed to him, another place he couldn't stand to be. His sitting room was already out of bounds, where Thomas Bettany had robbed him of . . . He couldn't list precisely what Bettany had stolen, but knew he was no longer the person he'd been. Once you'd faced torture, even if that torture never laid blade on skin, you were diminished. You knew the floor of your own fear, and how it felt to be dragged along its surface.

One drop of water won the race, and the other lost. Coe had forgotten which was which.

If he smashed the window, glass would go tumbling down onto passing strangers, leaving ears severed, lips like burst strawberries. Wounds blossomed whenever Coe closed his eyes. He couldn't walk into his sitting room without seeing it draped in black plastic.

He scrunched his hands and punched his cheeks. For hours he'd been unable to stir himself to life. The small time he'd not been brooding on Bettany, he'd been brooding on Dame Ingrid instead. Who had not only fed him to the cut-throat bastard, but had seen no evil in what she'd done.

You've had an upsetting experience.

Thanks. He'd worked that out.

If he'd killed you we'd have swept it under the carpet. You'd have been a random victim of city crime.

A few short days ago, admiring the view from Ingrid Tearney's office, he'd thought he was on the inside track. He understood now that he'd been chosen for precisely the opposite reason. Dame Ingrid, reaching for someone from one of the Service's lesser departments, had plucked the slightest nobody. When you're staking out bait for a tiger, you don't use your best goat.

And take the rest of the day off, he'd been told.

You don't look yourself. We all need a sick day now and then.

So he was expected to turn up tomorrow as if everything was normal.

He laid a hand flat against the window. Didn't punch but pushed gently, enough to feel the glass pushing back—to know that it was solid, and wouldn't give without effort. Even glass was capable of that much. And he remembered again how he'd shit himself when Bettany had stepped into view, naked, wielding a knife.

Enough. He grabbed his car keys from their hook. He wasn't sure where he was going, but simple movement might suffice. Perhaps he could lose himself on the grey streets, in the grey traffic. If he managed that much, he'd never have to turn up anywhere again.

The gunman had left by the towpath door, and by the time Bettany burst through it he'd vanished. Cramming the gun inside his coat, Bettany ran for the bridge.

On its near side a muddy slope between bushes led up to the road, a shortcut for kids. Bettany, taking it at a gallop, was two strides up when he lost his footing, and felt the air rush past as everything turned somersaults. He landed flat on his back, the breath knocked out of him, and the Makarov clattering on the towpath.

A young man stared at it in horror.

Bettany grabbed the gun and snarled, "Police." It came out a breathless gobbet. He shoved the Makarov out of sight and tried the slope again, his hands grabbing at spiny branches. His fingers were bloody when he reached the top, and there was no sign of his quarry. Behind him was a garbled alarm, a young man shouting into his phone. Bettany kept moving.

Cars lined the road. The gunman could be yards away, crouching behind a wheelbase, but Bettany didn't think so. Hiding places left you immobile. When the chance to run presented itself, you ran.

The street hit a main road a hundred yards ahead, and traffic criss-crossed the junction. Bettany jogged that way, conscious of the gun in his pocket, of the call being made on the towpath. A running man on a London street was someone to notice. He might as well be wearing a rhinestone jacket ... He stopped at the corner. Both pavements were busy, pedestrians ambling past or popping in and out of shops, queuing at bus stops, crowding the pedestrian lights on the next block. Still no quarry, which didn't mean he wasn't near. Bettany had pulled that trick himself—dumped a coat, affected a slouch, adjusted a collar. It could earn you two minutes' grace in a crowd.

Motionless, he tried to take in everything, alert for that tiny giveaway, the turned head, the altered speed. But there was nothing. A bus trundled past, stopped yards away, and disgorged more extras. In the distance a siren whined.

Bettany didn't bother with the slouch, or adjusting his collar. He didn't check the bus's destination either, but joined the queue boarding it, and allowed it to carry him away.

5.2

Never set off into city traffic without a plan in mind.

If you do, other drivers will hate you and try to kill you.

The third time he'd caused mass outrage by hesitating at a junction—the screaming of horns a mechanised fatwa—JK Coe thought he'd better choose a destination, even if he allowed the signage to dictate it.

East, something read.

If he drove far enough east he'd reach the sea. But even as the plan formulated it dissolved into spray, splashed into nothing, and he was passing another sign, and flashing his indicator far too late for the car behind him—

Another metal threat, spelt out in five blasts on a horn.

But he'd made his decision and was circling the roundabout, finding his exit.

N1.

Where Bettany's lair was, his late son's flat.

Two days ago, Coe had studied his file. It was no great feat of memory to dredge an address from it—doing research, assimilating information, reproducing it as required, was what he did.

Illegally, he fished his iPhone out and dropped it in his lap. Driving one-handed, he tapped to his streetfinder and entered the details.

Now he had a plan, the proof of it in front of him, a red line tracing a course through city streets, the way magic maps in children's storybooks did. Science was dragging old myths into everyday life—something to think about instead of thinking about what he was doing. Last night the monster had crawled into Coe's cave, and how had that worked out? But here Coe was, heading for the monster's own den. What was he going to do when he got there—ring its bell and run away?

Half his attention on the map, the rest of it all over the place, he nearly blew a red light and screeched to a halt a yard over the line.

The silence that greeted this reeked of contempt.

Waiting for the lights to turn, he took deep breaths and powered down to normal.

He was doing the research, he told himself.

Following which, he would assimilate the information.

If Bettany was there, which he might not be, nothing need come of it. Coe could still return home and spend the rest of the day, all the coming night, sitting in his stinking kitchen because his other rooms frightened him.

"Let's flag that up as option one," he said aloud.

His voice was flat and dull.

The lights went to green. He pulled off, following his iPhone's lead.

The road ahead split around a park, which serviced a three-block high-rise estate on its northern edge. To the other side lay a warren of streets, built around long-gone focal points. On one of them was Bettany's son's flat.

Going home was option one . . . But the lifelessness of his own voice was an argument against. Going home was giving up. He might as well cancel all plans for the future. All there'd be left for him would be the hollow construct of his own selfhood, which he'd have to learn to live inside. It would be like dressing himself in clothes three times too big.

If he didn't want to spend the rest of his life frightened, he had to do something today.

He'd arrived. It was a street of terraced rows twelve houses long and four storeys high, whose upper windows had small balconies bordered by wrought-iron railings. The window woodwork was white, but the front doors varied from green to purple to red. Coe drove slowly, as if looking for a parking space, and clocked the house he was after. Red door. He kept driving.

His antennae twitched.

Bettany's flat was being watched.

Flea said, "Well."

They were in the office with its new hole in the wall, a blank pupil staring vacantly out.

Boo Berryman, his temple a red mess, was weighing his mobile in his hand. He might have been preparing to throw it.

"What now?" he said.

Bettany had left on the run. The gunman was also in the wind. The Americanism seemed to fit. Gunmen in the office was not a British thing.

These thoughts were slow and muffled. Flea's recent history was blurring, as if viewed through smeary glass. But she'd remember fighting for air. She'd wake up some nights gasping, wrestling the pillows.

"We have to call the police," Boo said. "There were *guns*."

There was still a gun. Boo had put it on Vincent's desk.

Flea said, "This wasn't a random attack, you know. Not a passing lunatic. It was planned."

Driscoll said, "Somebody's mad because they think I'm giving away a fortune. Someone who's invested in the company."

"Someone who's powerful," Flea said.

"We could find out who," Boo said. "The shareholders . . ."

"Most of them are companies," Driscoll said. "Not individuals."

"Which makes it a job for the police," Boo said. "Am I the only one who remembers what just happened?"

Flea said, "He was a spy. Liam's father. That's the sort of people he knows, used to know. If the security service is behind this, what makes you think the police can be trusted?"

"Paranoid, much?"

"Well, yes. Just lately."

"Are you seriously saying we do nothing?"

Boo aimed the question at his boss.

Who said, "Maybe Flea's right. Maybe going to the police isn't a solution."

"People could get hurt," Boo said.

People already have been, thought Flea, touching her throat.

Driscoll said, "If Bettany was right, I'm the one in danger. And once *Shades 3*'s out, the danger goes away. The company can't reverse the release even if I'm dead."

"And what about that madman in the meantime? He's out there on the streets."

"Bettany will deal with him."

"It's Bettany I was talking about," said Boo.

5.3

Coe drove round a corner or two and parked by a church whose redbrick spire cast a shadow over its neighbours. A row of headstones out front had been weathered into illegibility, and a squirrel sat on one, twitching every few seconds like a furry metronome.

There was a half-full bottle of once-fizzy water in the well by the driver's seat, and Coe drained it, then sat drumming his fingers on its empty plastic.

There'd been four of them, in pairs. Two in a van with sliding doors, another two in a car at the next junction. Maybe he was wrong, and the area was a hotbed of men with no visible occupation, but it looked to Coe like a reception committee.

The van was for Bettany.

Coe thought, *I don't even have to lift a finger.*

The squirrel twitched once more, then jumped from the headstone and scampered up a tree.

Whoever they were, they were hostiles. Friendlies don't travel in packs.

They'll snatch him, pack him in the van. Do to him what he did to me, only for real.

Do you know what a professional would do? A professional would hurt you straight off the bat. Badly. To establish the perimeter.

There was a cracking noise as Coe crushed the plastic bottle in his fist.

The thought of Bettany reduced to a piece of meat . . .

It was payback. At a remove, so without risk. The crew watching Bettany's flat might not be top-rank, because Coe wouldn't have spotted them if they were, but they'd outweigh Bettany even if they didn't take him by surprise. Who they were, Coe neither knew nor cared. It was hardly a shock, to find there were others wishing Bettany harm. Motive didn't matter.

He dropped the bottle at his feet.

All that mattered was the outcome.

A group of children passed by in variations of a loosely applied uniform, grey or white shirts, dark trousers, dark skirts. Splashes of maroon on scarves and ties. A black girl, maybe twelve, glanced back at him and her eyes narrowed.

Oh, great, he thought. A lone man, parked near a school. He'd better move.

It was the first thought he'd had all day uncoloured by thoughts of Tom Bettany, and he was preparing to act on it when his phone rang.

Unknown caller.

"Coe," he said.

"It's me."

A greeting reserved for loved ones.

The car grew colder, as if a sudden snowfall had dumped on its roof.

"It's me," his caller repeated. "Bettany."

■   ■   ■

When Bishop got back from his errand to find the crew staking out Bettany's flat in high-vis formation, his first instinct was to use his new gadget on them, see how they liked being, what would you call it? Galvanised.

Not a metaphor in this instance, he'd have had to explain to them first. Not that they'd know what a metaphor was. Or even, possibly, an instance.

"So you don't think he's gunna clock you? Sitting in pairs, yards from his front door?"

The five of them in a huddle on the corner, two paying less attention to what Bishop had to say than to whatever they'd trodden their box-fresh trainers in.

"Or might he just leg it before you've noticed he's there?"

"He's an old guy, right? How fast can he run?"

The man who'd spoken—who called himself Freehold—had long hair tied back with a rubber band, carefully maintained stubble, and a leather jacket with fringing on the arms. He looked more like a talent-show hopeful than useful muscle, and the Martin Boyd Bishop remembered would have put him on the pavement without breaking stride.

And something about the way he'd said *old guy* carried the unspoken postscript *like you.*

"Let me put it this way," Bishop said.

Taking the stun gun from his pocket, he jammed it against Freehold's chest and pulled the trigger.

Dancer Blaine had said, "It's top of the range. Better than what the blues are using, even."

"Sure it is."

But Blaine had insisted.

"That's security service issue, that is."

Which was just Blaine's way of adding a zero to the price, because how would he get hold of top class gear like that? But the fact was he had what Bishop needed, which was a way of putting Boyd down without killing him.

Security service issue. Didn't sound likely.

Impressive piece of kit though, because Freehold hit the deck like his strings had been cut. Went from a smirk to a smear in less time than it took to strike a match.

"Get him in the van," he told them. "Park it round the corner. And take the car down past the junction."

Bishop tucked the stun gun away.

"And when he comes round, tell him old guys have their moments."

5.4

"**Y**ou still there?"

"How'd you get this number?"

Bettany didn't reply.

And Coe didn't need him to, because the answer was obvious. His clothes in a pile in his bedroom, like a suicide's on a beach. Wallet and phone on top.

He said, "What do you want?"

"You reported back to Tearney, didn't you?"

"What do you want?" he repeated.

"And she cut you loose. Told you to go home and keep quiet."

Coe said nothing.

"Hurts, doesn't it? It's eating away at you. I can hear it in your voice."

Coe trapped his tongue between his teeth, and bit down hard.

"It wasn't personal. You know that."

And now he couldn't help himself.

"So this is what, an apology? You're calling to say sorry?"

"I did what I had to do," Bettany said. "More to the point, I did what she knew I'd do. She set you up, buddy."

"I know."

"Of course you know. So what are you doing now? My guess is, one of two things."

Again, he bit his tongue.

"You're either cowering in your flat, scared of the whole world. Or you're out pretending to look for me."

". . . Pretending?"

"We both know you don't want to find me. So where are you? By Liam's flat?"

Coe didn't answer.

"Figures. Because that's where I'm least likely to be, isn't it? In case I'm wrong and Tearney does release the hounds."

Coe thought of the men he'd spotted, and said nothing.

"You still there?"

"Third time. What do you want?"

"Same as you. To settle a debt."

"My debt's with you."

"No. It's with her. You were collateral damage. You going to blame the gun or the woman who fired it?"

Coe said nothing.

Bettany said, "She told you it was for the good of the Service, right?"

Why did you join, she'd asked.

Sense of duty, desire to serve.

"Well, she was lying. It's about money, Coe. She wanted Vincent Driscoll dead because she's a shareholder in his company, and he's about to drive it off a cliff. Nothing to do with defence of the realm. She wanted a cut-rate assassin."

Coe thought of designer suits fading at the seams. Of a thread pulling loose at a collar.

It was about money.

"How long have you known?" he asked.

"Almost from the start. You know about the Zombie List?"

It was a list of all those who weren't quite dead yet. Anyone who'd been in the Service was on the Zombie List, and anyone on the Zombie List rang bells when they bumped into officialdom.

"Well, I'm not on it. Or the police would have known who I was. Back when they told me Liam was dead."

Coe remembered saying as much to Dame Ingrid.

You know what records are like, she'd said. *We don't need him setting off unnecessary alarm bells.*

"She said it was some ... She suggested it was a bureaucratic balls-up."

"Sure she did. But it was deliberate. She didn't want me on the radar, not while she was prepping me to kill Driscoll."

"Which you didn't."

"No. But she'd planned for that too."

Something slapped on the car roof and Coe's heart flipped over. A group of kids were pelting down the pavement, laughing like hyenas.

"... You still there?"

"Why are you telling me this?"

"Why do you think?"

"You want something."

"Everybody wants something, Coe. They didn't get round to that module yet? In Psych Eval?"

"What do you want? No—what was her back-up plan?"

"She sent someone else to kill him. Maybe she planned to hang it on me, I don't know. But this guy, he's been in the picture a while, keeping tabs on me. He was at Liam's funeral."

The phone throbbed silently in Coe's hand.

"He probably killed my son."

Liam. There hadn't even been a picture of him in Bettany's file. His death had started this, but he'd become wallpaper. He was like the leaky pipe that caused the flood. Once it started, you forgot about the pipe. You concentrated on the flood.

It was important to remember that this wasn't the case for Bettany.

Coe said, "Did he kill Driscoll?"

"No. But he got away."

"What do you want, Bettany?"

"You know what I want."

"She's the head of the Service, for Christ's sake."

"She's the woman who had my son killed so I'd commit a murder."

"So you're going to what, kill her instead? You won't last five minutes."

"And that bothers you?"

Coe didn't reply.

So Tearney had primed Bettany, he thought, and aimed him like a gun, pointing him at Driscoll by having Coe warn him off, which was the kind of backwards-thinking she specialised in. It hadn't worked, but she'd had a back-up plan—she'd always have a back-up plan, and another one behind that. Wander far enough into her machinations and you'd meet yourself coming back. Just as puzzled, just as lost.

He said, "What about the other one?"

"What other one?"

"The drugs guy. Marten Saar."

Now it was Bettany's turn to say nothing.

Coe said, "He was the alternative target. Do you really think Tearney plucked him from a hat? If he was the decoy, there was a reason."

"He's responsible for muskrat. Which Liam was smoking when he fell. Was pushed."

"That's what they told you he was smoking. To put Saar in the frame."

Hearing himself say the words, he wondered if he even believed them. But it didn't matter. They might be true.

He thought of the men watching the flat. Maybe Tom Bettany would never return there—maybe he was already in a flight pattern, one act of vengeance short of heading back for the shadows—but if he did, maybe they'd take him.

And once he was in that van, it'd be his turn to find out who worked with meat.

Bettany said, "You might have a point. But that's not what I'm after."

So Coe told him where he could find Dame Ingrid Tearney.

After ending the call Bettany sat on St. Paul's steps, thinking. The steps were stone cold, damp rising up through them, but he wasn't the only one squatting there. Tourists surrounded him, mostly kids in bright-coloured rainwear, sharing lunches from plastic boxes. At any given moment, half of them were filming the others on their phones. The spaces in London where unrecorded life went on were few and far between. Something he needed to keep in mind, now the McGarry crew knew he was back in town.

His own phone wouldn't take a picture, let alone a movie, but it would get the job done.

He rang Bad Sam Chapman once more. Waiting for an answer, he watched an Italian teenager preening for a camera, glowing with health and good looks, and an unironic awareness of both. Then a weary-toned Chapman asked, "What is it this time?"

"Tell me more about Oskar Kask," he said.

5.5

Late afternoon and, even twenty-two storeys up, light had leached from the sky. Through glass streaked with the residue of dirty rain Marten Saar looked down on Hackney's many lights, some moving, some stationary, and some the one while seeming the other—streetlights glimpsed through waving branches flickering hither and yon. Saar's day was just beginning, which meant the West End, deals, meetings, setting in motion the diplomatic machinery to initiate contact with the Cousins' Circle. That was Oskar Kask's job, and Oskar had phoned to say he'd meet Marten at the club. Asked where he'd been all day he'd given a wolfish snigger, suggestive of satisfied appetites.

Which Saar had echoed with one of his own.

Now he was dressed, alone in the expanse of the L-shaped room. His crew were elsewhere on the floor, supervising the weighing and bagging of product, activities performed in the main by women from the Old Country, or else watching *The Sopranos*, to which they'd become addicted. Which was fine by Saar. If he needed anyone—

The door opened and a body fell through it.

It was followed by a tall blond man Saar had never laid eyes on before.

The man stepped inside, closing the door behind him.

Saar said, "Is this a joke?"

His voice was commendably calm in the circumstances, though he knew his accent sounded thicker than usual.

"Depends," said the stranger. "Is this your best man?"

He meant Lepik, who until recently had been on lobby duty, an undemanding task involving making sure nobody used Saar's lift.

Looking big was usually as much as this took.

Saar said, "Not really."

The man looked round. "How many others?"

Saar shook his head.

"Five? Six?"

"Seven," Saar said.

"More than I can handle."

Saar shrugged. "I can't tell yet. Are you armed?"

"Uh-huh."

"Then I expect you'll account for a few of them."

"Automatic weapons?"

"This will make you laugh," Saar said. "One of my boys? He has an anti-tank gun."

"That's got to come in handy," the man said.

"That's what he tells me."

"In Hackney."

Saar laughed without making a noise, and mimed a bazooka-shape at the intruder. "Boom," he said. Then he wafted the air, as if walking through mist, before laughing silently again and dropping his hands to his trouser pockets.

"Where I can see them?"

"Ah, yes. Because you are . . . armed."

The man opened his coat, showing Saar the handle of a gun.

Marten Saar took his hands from his pockets.

He said, "I raise my voice and out they come."

"I'm sure."

"Ever vigilant."

"Like this guy."

Saar said, "Him, I'll have to have words with."

"Maybe later."

Saar wondered whether to try for his phone again, nestled in his trouser pocket, but the intruder gave a slight shake of his head, and he decided not to. If this man had come to kill him, Saar knew he would be dead already. But there was no sense pushing his luck.

He said, "We haven't been introduced."

"I'm guessing you're Marten Saar."

"Which gives you—what's the phrase?—the advantage."

The man laughed. "I have a gun. You haven't. Yes, I'd call that having the advantage. But just to even things up, you can call me Boyd."

"And what is it you want, Mr. Boyd?"

"We need to talk about Oskar," Tom Bettany said.

The club was one they used often, as was Marten's line about the VIP enclosure, and the second-best application of a velvet rope. Oskar Kask usually made the effort to smile when he delivered it. One of the burdens of non-leadership.

But Marten was late tonight. Oskar was on his own, bottle of beer in front of him. Earlier he'd put away half a pint of vodka, but that had been an emergency. In his flat near Farringdon station, his secret bolt-hole, he'd swallowed a three-ounce measure without blinking before showering away the morning's sweat, not all of it due to exertion. He could smell fear on his skin, its sheen glazing his neck. Twenty minutes under thundering water, the last five minutes freezing cold, was almost enough to wash it away. Draining the rest of the bottle almost finished the job.

Oskar's instructions had been clear enough. If Bettany didn't waste Driscoll, he was to step in and do it himself—you didn't have to spend much time with Dame Ingrid to learn that she never made a plan without wrapping it round a smaller one. Bettany, she'd assured him, would wind up in the frame anyway, not that that mattered to Oskar.

But then Bettany had appeared out of nowhere, and come within an ace of taking him down.

He took a pull on his beer, the bottle's neck cold on his teeth. Being late wasn't one of Marten's usual faults, the worst of which was a tendency to cast himself as romantic visionary. Not long ago it had just been the pair of them, squeezing a living from a fraction of a postcode, Marten not the brain he thought he was, but with a knack of convincing others there was more to him than a thug on the make. His self-belief had pulled them out of the shallow end, and Oskar had loved him for that. But once muskrat took off, complications arose. One of these took the shape of Clem Baker, a wannabe lord of the universe—or that section of it currently occupied by Marten Saar and Oskar Kask—and it had become necessary for Oskar to put a bullet in his head, which was doubly unfortunate. Unfortunate for Baker, of course, but a pain in the arse for Oskar too, because he'd forgotten the cardinal rule of shooting people during peacetime, which was not to get caught afterwards.

Though as things turned out, that had turned out to be an opportunity too. Thank you, Dame Ingrid, he said silently, clinking his bottle against the edge of the table before draining it.

Still no sign of Marten.

He raised a finger, and another bottle was brought.

And right there in a nutshell, that was what he liked. The crook of a finger that brought results. The knowledge that someone within bottleshot was waiting to satisfy his needs, simply because he was Oskar Kask. A long way from the lucky hustler working corners. Not so important yet he didn't have to laugh at other people's jokes, but time wrought changes. Nothing stayed the same forever.

He realised that the object he was turning over in his left hand was the blue plastic lighter. He raised it up and clicked the ignition a time or two, but it wouldn't spark. He slipped it out of sight.

Oskar loved Marten, but time wrought changes, and Oskar wasn't going to be laughing at the same unfunny lines forever. There'd still be somebody tugging his strings, but at least Dame Ingrid was a silent partner. She wouldn't expect him to laugh at her jokes.

From the same pocket he'd produced the lighter, Oskar fished out his phone.

Time to find out where Marten had got to.

His visitor had gone.

Through the window a southbound jumbo winked in and out of vision, defined by the lights on its tail and wings, and heading for somewhere distant.

Marten Saar would have liked to be on that plane.

Burdens of leadership, though. You stood your ground and made tough decisions.

He remembered Oskar telling him that, as recently as last week. (Oskar, whom he trusted with his life. But trust needed daily renewal.) Oskar had been prepping him, if that was the word he meant—Oskar had been *priming* him on this alliance business, drip drip dripping like a tap. You didn't even notice it at the time. But that was what it was like, a dripping effect, water on stone. Sooner or later, the stone crumbled. Always, water won.

. . . Oskar, who had stood shoulder-to-shoulder with him during the lean years, but had lately taken to saying *Sure, boss?* when he should have been saying *Sure, boss.*

The visitor had called himself Martin Boyd, and it didn't matter if that was his real name or one he'd pulled on for the occasion. What mattered was, he'd been telling the truth.

If Oskar was here, he'd lay some grief on Marten for that.

"A stranger shows, you lap up every word? Because what, he has an honest face?"

Well, yes, no. Maybe. Marten had seen honester faces, if you wanted to get particular.

No, what had convinced him was the familiarity of the information, as if Boyd had been reminding him of something he'd already known, but had decided not to pay attention to. Like a domestic inconvenience. A squeaky hinge that you never got round to oiling, because ninety-nine hundredths of the time, it didn't matter. Ninety-nine hundredths of the time, you weren't using the hinge, so it wasn't squeaking.

Until somebody points out that you've got a problem, everything's fine.

Another question was, why was he still alone? His crew should be here, ready to take him to the club. Instead they were all watching *The Sopranos*, while for all they knew he was out here having his throat cut.

Well, not quite alone.

Lepik, breathing fitfully, still lay where Boyd had dropped him.

There was a large glass ashtray on a windowsill and Marten tapped his Marlboro into it thoughtfully.

Then he hurled it at the wall.

A moment later the boys came tumbling in, alert as a pack of spaniels, and equally effective.

"Boss—?"

"Shut up!"

The L-shaped space shivered with the echo as it bounced off windows and walls. And then everything was quiet, and then his phone rang.

This he also hurled against a wall, and watched it shatter.

"Things have been getting slack," he told his crew, speaking slowly, and in their own language.

He crossed the room, and stood over the recumbent Lepik.

"They've been getting lax."

He kicked Lepik in the stomach, as hard as he could.

"I pay you well, I raise your status, and what happens?"

He kicked Lepik in the crotch, as hard as he could.

"You become a bunch of lazy cretins. You dishonour me and you dishonour yourselves."

He circled the unconscious man as he spoke, without looking down at him. He was looking at the lazy cretins instead, who were busy avoiding his gaze, studying their feet or a patch of ceiling, or anything, though also not Lepik.

Whom Marten kicked in the back now, as hard as he could.

"But from tonight, things are going to be different. From tonight, you earn your keep. You understand?"

He kicked Lepik in the head, as hard as he could.

"I said, do you understand?"

They understood. They all understood, except Lepik, who was

losing whatever capacity for independent thought he'd ever possessed.

"Good."

He kicked Lepik in the face, as hard as he could.

A phone rang, but it wasn't Marten Saar's.

"Answer it, moron."

A phone was produced, answered, handed to Saar.

"It's Oskar."

"Oskar," said Marten. "No, I've had it switched off. I'm fine. A few press-ups, that's all. You're at the club? I'll be there. Ten minutes."

He ended the call and threw the phone at its owner. "Go fetch Oskar," he told him. "Bring him back here. You too."

"Boss."

The nominated pair left, and Marten kicked Lepik in the head again. Then he swore loudly in several languages and kicked Lepik again, then again, and kept kicking him until the sweat soaked through to his jacket. Only then did he stop.

He was damp and panting.

His shoes were a mess.

The rest of his crew were studiedly not watching, their gazes fixed anywhere but on their boss, and what used to be their colleague.

Marten jerked a thumb over his shoulder. "Get rid of that," he said.

He went to get changed.

Behind him his men began prising up a section of carpet, folding it carefully so its contents didn't spill.

5.6

Bettany had gone to earth, avoiding the obvious places—transport hubs and cheap flophouses. Instead he'd taken the Metropolitan line to the suburbs and found a Travelodge. Back in the city, the Brothers McGarry's crew would be flexing its fingers by now, poking them into all the local holes. The brothers themselves wouldn't be seeing unwalled daylight for years, but their business would be trundling on, their old gangboss, Bishop, calling the shots. He'd be keen on meeting Martin Boyd again too. Boyd had robbed him of years of his life.

All that time in the shadows, hiding from himself as much as from anyone else, and here he was back again, stirring up old enemies and making new ones too. Nobody walks away, though. Everyone comes home in the end, one way or another.

He'd bought a takeaway which he ate sitting on the bed, watching the news. A minor story, relegated to local events, was a police action in N1 after a witness claimed to have seen an armed man. A Met spokesman explained that all such reports were treated with the utmost seriousness. If anyone saw a man with a gun, they should call the police immediately.

Bettany turned it off.

Oskar Kask had got away, but wouldn't be on the loose long. He too would have to go home sometime, and Bettany had poisoned the well for him there. If his undercover years had taught him anything, it was that everyone expects to be betrayed. Marten Saar had bought his story as if he'd long since paid the deposit. Kask could look over his shoulder all he wanted, but Bettany had arranged for him to be flattened from the front.

He disposed of the food cartons, rinsed his mouth, undressed and got under the covers. But lying in the dark, the nearby traffic strangely comforting, Bettany found himself thinking about Martin Boyd again, the man he'd been for almost a decade. It was a strange trick, being someone else. Undercover was only half about remembering who you were supposed to be, it was mostly about forgetting who you were. Boyd came back to him in dreams even now, dreams freighted with memories of betrayal and grief, and when he woke he was never sure who these emotions were for, those into whose friendship Boyd had crept like a lizard, and who doubtless still cursed him from their cells, or for Hannah, for Liam, the loved ones from the life he lived when he was pretending to be Thomas Bettany. It was too late to know the difference any more, and neither Hannah nor Liam were there to tell him ...

A jolt pulled him back from sleep, like a misstep from a pavement. Liam's ashes. For a whole night Bettany had carried them round Hoxton, and their absence caused him to stumble now. They were back in the flat. Even as he had the thought, the disjunction struck him, that the ashes were *they* rather than *he*. They, Liam, were back in the flat.

So he would fetch them and scatter them on the river. That was his last conscious thought before sleep, that he would scatter his son's ashes on the Thames, but when he woke in the night it wasn't from a dream of Liam but of Majeed, with whom he'd worked in Marseilles, and with whom he'd found a peculiar kind of friendship. Peculiar because Bettany had neither sought nor welcomed friendship these past few years. Survival had seemed enough to be getting on with. The dream had concerned betrayal, but the details slipped from meaning even before he opened his eyes.

He closed them again, but there was no more sleep that night.

Oskar finished his beer and slipped out for a smoke. When he returned the bottle had been replaced by a fresh one and the girl responsible, he thought her name was Anita, winked to make sure he knew who to tip.

Anita. Maybe Annette. Something like that.

Still no Marten.

He sat with hands flat, fingers spread wide. Even when he raised them they stayed steady. It had been a close-run thing, but history didn't read match reports, it just gave the result. Oskar had dealt with many problems but this was the first time he'd gone up against a professional—Bettany had been a spy, and spies receive training dope peddlers don't get. So Oskar could clap himself on the back for being here at the club, a beer in front of him, and not dead on a towpath.

Halfway through these thoughts two men approached.

Zac and Karu.

No Marten.

Oskar leaned back.

"You took your time."

"There's been a change of plan," Zac said.

"What change?"

"We're meeting back at the flat."

"Why?"

Karu said, "Because Marten said so."

"Okay, sure," Oskar said. "Let me just finish my beer."

He smiled lazily, reached for the bottle, and broke it on Karu's forehead, then wiped the remnant across Zac's face. While Zac wept blood, Oskar walked calmly to the exit. As he stepped outside, the noise behind him was swelling to a roar.

"What's happening?" the nearest smoker asked.

Oskar turned the collar of his jacket up against the cold. "Didn't see."

At the corner he hailed a cab.

"Where to?"

"Farringdon Road."

Settling back, he wondered how Marten had found out, then dismissed the question as irrelevant. All that mattered was what happened next. And while Marten was supposedly the brains, it didn't take Oskar more than half a minute to collate a few bullet points.

Back to the bolt-hole.

Collect spare gun.

Find Marten.

Shoot him.

After that, everything was back on track.

The crew wouldn't be a problem, having worked with Oskar as long as they had with Marten. They wouldn't be swearing blood oaths, they'd be shrugging shoulders, and by morning they'd have fallen in line.

Well, maybe not Zac and Karu.

As for the Driscoll business, Dame Spook would have to find some other way of sealing that deal. Oskar would concentrate on locking down the business with the Cousins' Circle, enough to keep her happy.

The taxi pulled over to give a whooping police car, its busy blue light bouncing off nearby windows, room to scrape past.

Oskar checked his pockets for his wallet, hoping he hadn't left it behind in his hurry. It was there, though a second check of the same pockets revealed that the blue plastic lighter wasn't. It didn't matter. It couldn't be used to identify him. It wasn't even his.

"Here's fine," he said, when Farringdon station's new facade came into view. He paid the driver, and stepped out into damp night air.

5.7

When Flea opened her eyes she was assailed by unfamiliar shapes. No—she was assailed by familiar shapes in unfamiliar configurations. There was a wardrobe and a curtained window. There was a door. There was the foot of the bed she was lying on. Nothing unusual, but not her own bedroom.

Waking in a strange bed wasn't an entirely new experience, but she didn't make a habit of it. On this occasion, anyway, she was alone.

No light penetrated the curtains. It could have been ten at night or two in the morning.

And then the day's details returned to her in one big information dump, and she groaned softly. On her breath she could taste the brandy she'd been given "for the shock" when they'd arrived at Vincent's, and the second she'd drunk largely for the taste, and the third because . . . well, because. She recalled her knees giving way, as the morning's tension resolved itself in a moment of utter liquidity. The arm wrapped round her throat was there again, and people were pointing guns at her. She remembered being carried somewhere, presumably to this very bed, but could not remember who by. She pondered that for a moment or two, then groaned again, and pulled herself upright.

She was fully clothed, thank God, but could not find her shoes. Her bag, too, was presumably downstairs. And it occurred to her that having a violent stranger seize her was perhaps not the most dangerous thing to happen to her today, because here she was after dark, in Vincent's spare bedroom, and how well did she know him? Boo Berryman too, come to that? Wasn't there something odd about the pair of them, living together in this half-hidden house? And why hadn't either of them thought to leave a glass of water on the bedside table?

Driven by thirst, she padded out of the room as quietly as she could, onto a dark landing. There was a vague illumination from downstairs, a flickering light laid on by the special effects department of whatever spooky film this was. Anyone could be lurking down there. This morning, when Tom Bettany had chased the gunman out onto the towpath—at that moment it had seemed like it was all over, the mad plot she'd fallen into after Liam had died. Now, she wasn't so sure.

The stair creaked, and the noise echoed downstairs, as if someone had shifted on hearing her approach.

Flea froze.

The sound was not repeated.

How had she ended up here, anyway? It seemed as good a time as any to ask that question.

Because of Liam, she decided. It was because she had been friends with Liam Bettany, who, for a while—if she were honest with herself—she had thought might be a prospective partner, but who had proved too unfocused, too unsuccessful, too broke. And so she had turned her attention to her boss, Vincent Driscoll. For a while now, she had entertained a fantasy of drawing Vincent out of his shell, dragging him from the hide-away he'd constructed for himself. This would be a challenge. The fact that he was rich didn't hurt. But right this minute, what she was mostly remembering was how, when Tom Bettany had aimed the gun at him, Vincent had seemed preternaturally calm. Even for a man set at an angle to everyday emotions, wasn't that a little scary?

The flickering light, she realised, came from a fire.

There were only two ways to go, up and down. So she went on down, into the large room that constituted most of the ground floor of Vincent's bachelor house.

Her eyes had grown accustomed to the gloom now, but even so it took a moment to locate him. He sat on one end of a wide sofa at the far end of the room, and in the firelight looked other-worldly. His skin wasn't fair so much as faint, as if she might prod right through him, were she so inclined. His body would ripple round her finger like a reflection.

The glass of red wine he held had either been filled very full to start with or he'd made no serious inroads yet.

Her shoes and her bag lay on the floor by an armchair. Next to them, a half-filled brandy glass.

She approached warily, unsure how this was going to develop, and because he didn't speak, she found she had to.

"You're still up."

Mentally, she awarded herself a state-the-bleeding-obvious prize for this.

"I seem to have been in bed," she went on.

He said, "I know. I carried you there."

"Oh." Her mind flapped around for a fuller response, and possibly her mouth did too, but in the end all she could manage was, "So . . . What are you doing?"

"Just thinking."

"I'm sorry to interrupt . . ."

"I'd finished."

"Oh."

She didn't know how to pick up from this. Thinking, to her mind, was something you did more or less continually. Sitting with a glass of wine, staring at a fire, you were almost certainly deep in thought. Even if the thoughts were shapeless and inexact, they remained thoughts—there was nothing else for them to be.

He said, "I had an idea."

She realised that it wasn't only the firelight that was making his eyes gleam. The gleaming was coming from within. For the first time she could recall, she was seeing Vincent Driscoll lit by his own being.

Forgetting her need for water, she sank onto the sofa.

"Tell me about it," she said.

Oskar's Farringdon bolt-hole, the one nobody knew about, was up a flight of stairs, through a dirty front door sandwiched between a dry cleaners and an electrical goods shop that had whitewashed its windows the previous week. He headed up in darkness and went straight for the bedroom where he kept his spare gun in a shoebox on top of the wardrobe.

The shoebox was there, but the Glock had gone.

He blinked twice.

The gun remained absent.

Then he closed the box thoughtfully, almost mournfully, knowing the time for panicking was over.

The time for panicking had been back in the club, when Marten was late. Because Marten was never late.

Oskar stepped into the living room, and turned the light on.

Marten sat in the armchair, Oskar's gun in one hand, and a cigarette in the other that he lit as soon as Oskar appeared.

"That's better," he said.

Blue smoke drifted ceilingwards.

He waggled the Glock as if it were his finger.

"Don't bother getting comfortable. We're not staying."

Oskar asked, "How long have you known?"

"About this place? Since five minutes after you picked up the keys. About the rest of it, the alliance we make with the Cousins' Circle so you can inform on their activities to the British secret service? Not so long."

"Bettany," said Oskar.

"He told me his name was Boyd."

Marten tapped ash onto a carpet frayed colourless.

"And that he was supposed to kill me. And that if he didn't, you would."

"You can't have believed him."

"Can't I? Why can't I do that, Oskar?"

"We've been partners forever."

"Which means neither of us could ever betray the other, is that right? Please—"

This in response to Oskar opening his mouth, about to say something.

"—don't insult me with a fairytale. If nothing else, we've been partners too long for that."

Oskar didn't know what he'd have said, if he'd had the chance to say it. But yes, it would have been a fairytale.

For half a minute they remained silent. Not far away there was music, the kind whose unrelenting beat is its entire point, and the irritation it causes to anyone over thirty a mere bonus. It came from a club, perhaps, or a pub jukebox, or a nearby flat.

It came from somewhere where people listened in the full expectation that this was just another night they were living through, which would give way in turn to another day, and so on. And so on.

The door at the bottom of the stairs opened.

Oskar said, "One favour?"

Marten tilted his head to one side like an interested bird.

"Do it here. Now. Quickly."

Marten shook his head.

Behind Oskar, more of Marten's crew arrived.

"Let's go home," said Marten.

5.8

It had rained hard in the early hours, bringing small branches down from trees, and while it was calmer now, with a hint of brightness in corners of the sky, pavements were still wet, and minor floods pooled at kerbside corners where leaves blocked the drains. At the entrance to the tube station the tiled floors were filthy with tracked-in dirt, and plastic warning triangles emblazoned with exclamation marks provided extra trip hazards. Coming in from the streets, back in Central London, Bettany felt that this almost-quaint station, sprouting like a redbrick mushroom in the middle of a constant traffic jam, was a time capsule, with its framed posters of bygone travelling experiences. But the thought didn't stay. He passed through the barriers and took the stairs to the platform two at a time.

The LED display suggested an incoming tube. A newspaper on a bench fluttered its pages in confirmation.

The train piled into the station as if it had no intention of stopping.

It did, though. Bettany sat on the bench, apparently studying the paper, while passengers disembarked. Ingrid Tearney wasn't among them, but he hadn't expected her. He was early.

Those waiting boarded the train and it creaked, then thundered, into the tunnel again.

He was alone on the platform.

Which was monitored, everyone knew this. But unless times had changed, people with nowhere to go haunted the underground, seeking warmth on its platforms, variety on its circuits, charity in its carriages. There was nothing unusual about a man passing time while the trains roared by. He wouldn't raise alarms.

The paper was a free handout, its news two cycles old. It didn't matter. He was scanning his surroundings, not the print.

If there was anyone else doing the same, they were too good to be spotted.

He folded the paper, tucked it under an arm, and leaned back into the bench's alcove. The LED warned of another approaching train.

The same routine. No Ingrid Tearney.

"She's the head of the Intelligence Service," JK Coe had told him. "You can't just sandbag her on the underground."

"I suspect she'll be expecting me," Bettany had said.

But what difference that would make, he wasn't sure. Legend suggested that she made her morning commute unaccompanied, but legend would suggest that, wouldn't it?

Another train. This time he stood, pursed his lips, looked like a man about to make a decision. It slowed to a halt, then jerked forward another yard and halted again. The doors opened. Passengers spilt onto the platform. Behind them, Dame Ingrid patiently waited her turn.

He stepped on board before she could depart, earning scowls

and passive-aggressive mutterings, and caught her by the arm before the crush had dissipated.

"A message from Driscoll," he said, bending to her ear. "He's calling a shareholders' meeting."

Her arm felt rigid in his grip.

A young woman leant forward. "Is this man bothering you? Why are you holding her like that?"

"He's an old friend," Ingrid Tearney said as Bettany released her. "But thank you for asking, my dear. Too few people worry about others."

The doors closed, and the train pulled away.

They did not speak for five minutes, during which the train stopped twice more and the young woman—still glowering at Bettany—disembarked. Seats became briefly available, and they sat.

Sitting on a crowded tube was to become child-sized again, on a level with the hips and stomachs of adults.

In a conversational tone, Dame Ingrid Tearney said, "Following me?"

"Waiting for you."

Her eyebrows narrowed.

"This is the carriage nearest your exit."

Dame Ingrid Tearney gave the smallest of nods.

"It's hard," she said, "not to fall into habits."

"You were never in the field."

She patted his knee.

"But I'm full of admiration for those of you who were."

A young man in a grey hoodie sitting opposite was gazing at them through the thicket of swaying bodies. But whatever he was earbudded to was consuming his attention.

Bettany said, "You recruited Oskar Kask last year, I'm guessing. After he was arrested for shooting a gangbanger."

"We'd been awaiting some such opportunity. Not that we'd had to wait long. You're aware of how it works. Violent men don't *resort* to violence. It's simply what they do."

She spoke quietly, as did he. Here in the middle of the throng, most of whose bodies were willing themselves elsewhere with laptops and iPods and Kindles, their conversation murmured on unheard.

"But Kask was perfect because he was placed to give you something you wanted. A way into the Cousins' Circle."

"A commendable target, I'm sure you agree."

"But too much trouble to actually infiltrate."

"Deep undercover? Too expensive. You were one of a dying breed, Mr. Bettany. And no offence, but really. A years-long operation? To take a handful of hoods off the streets? These aren't the returns we need these days."

"I'm sure," he said. "But this was unofficial, wasn't it?"

The train began to slow.

"Are we staying on?" she asked.

"End of the line."

The train stopped, and the doors opened.

Dame Ingrid said, "I have to tread a careful path. The good of the Service, versus the deniability of my lords and masters. Kask was too good an opportunity to miss. But he was also a murderer. Recruiting him was never going to be a popular move."

"But you did it anyway."

"As I say. Too good an opportunity to miss."

"Which meant when it came to going really off the books," Bettany said, "you had a ready-made tool to hand."

■   ■   ■

During the night, abandoned by sleep, he had etched patterns of vengeance on the hotel ceiling while his heartbeat became percussive. But now he was here, next to this calm woman who had ordered his son's death simply to draw him into her machinations, he found that he, too, was calm, as if he'd come through the hurricane's rage to find an unnatural stillness at its centre.

As for Dame Ingrid, nothing rattled her. The placidity of her ugliness—her iron-grey hairpiece, the putty-like growth on her nose's left flank—was its own disguise, within which she could fume and scheme unnoticed. That would have been a lesson she learned long before the Secret Service beckoned her.

Directly opposite them, the young man nodded to his iPod's beat.

Too obvious, thought Bettany. Too obvious.

He said, "Of course, it would have helped if I'd killed Marten Saar. Putting Oskar Kask in the driver's seat."

Dame Ingrid said, "It really doesn't matter to me. It mattered to Oskar, of course. He'd much rather have been in charge."

Mattered, thought Bettany.

He said, "But that was Plan B, wasn't it? Plan A being that I kill Vincent Driscoll. Of the two targets you set up, that was the one you were really after. Because that was for your own benefit, not the Service's."

Dame Ingrid barked, which turned out to be her way of laughing.

"You think this is funny?"

"Of course not, Mr. Bettany. But something frightfully amusing did just occur to me. I had this sudden thought that maybe you were recording this conversation as a way of gathering evidence."

The inverted commas she draped round "evidence" were heavy as curtains.

"And I was just counting the ways in which that would turn out to be a bad idea."

Bettany said, "You think you're fireproof. Are you bulletproof too, I wonder?"

"Really, Mr. Bettany. You should hear yourself. Threatening to shoot an old lady."

"You're the one who decided I was a violent man. What did you think was going to happen once I found out who really killed Liam?"

And there it was, out in the open.

She patted his knee again.

"I haven't had a chance to tell you how sorry I am about that. Marten Saar has a lot to answer for. Drugs do so much harm to young people."

He couldn't speak. This took his breath away.

"Mr. Coe suggested that you might blame yourself, and I do hope he's wrong about that. But psychology is such an unforgiving science."

The train slowed.

"Maybe you're right," he said abruptly.

"I'm not sure I follow."

"Maybe we should get off."

5.9

They were far from the centre now, way out east, in streets that were memory-haunted for Tom Bettany, or for Martin Boyd. Round here the Brothers McGarry had once held sway. You could still drop their name in any pub and expect a nod of recognition.

He had not given this a thought when leaving the tube, but looked round now automatically.

She said, "You're looking to see if we've been followed."

For a moment Bettany thought she'd been sharing his memories. Then he realised she meant her own security detail.

He said, "The coat you're wearing. It's seen better days."

"For a man whose tailor is a sweat-shop infant, you're very free with your criticism."

"I don't care about clothes. You do. You're broke, aren't you? That's why you want Driscoll dead."

She said, "It's been a difficult few years. I've always been shrewd in my investments, or so I thought. It turns out that perhaps I was merely lucky."

"And the luck ran out."

"And the luck ran out."

"That must have been tough."

She said, "He was planning on scuppering his own company. Giving away a product which was the main reason I'd invested in him in the first place."

"Killing him is hardly a long-term strategy. From the company's point of view."

Words rang like a chipped bell in his head. He was talking to the woman who'd had his son murdered. Her motive, lurking several layers deep, was only money. Liam, who had no money, had been killed so she might stay rich.

She said, "It would have solved my immediate problems. Without Driscoll, the shareholders would have reversed his fatheaded decision. The first two versions of his game made millions. There's no reason why the third shouldn't either."

"And you wanted me to do it for you."

"That would have been helpful."

"And that's why you had Liam killed."

His calmness as brittle now as a frosted leaf. Here in full view of the world, he might reach out and snap her neck.

But she'd come to a halt by a parked delivery van while a man brushed past her, manoeuvring a stack of plastic pallets from which new-baked smells were drifting.

"Good lord," she said. "Of course not. What do you take me for?"

If he was ambushing anyone else, thought Bishop, he'd have made himself comfortable in the boy's flat. There was no knowing how long it would be before Bettany returned to claim his son's ashes, and he didn't want to spend the time huddled on a bench, stamping feet against the cold. He could commandeer the van, but passing officials tended to notice men sitting in vans, and the world was full of officials these days, community-support noddies and revenue ambassadors, or whatever traffic wardens were called this week. He didn't want to end up on some peaked-cap wearer's mobile phone gallery, suspicious character #101. And he had low tolerance for jobsworths asking questions.

But the flat was no-go. Bettany was not an amateur. He'd moulded himself into the McGarrys' crew and had kept up that pretence for years, which meant he must have developed a sixth sense for all manner of disturbance. If Bishop was in the flat when he entered, he'd know it before he'd closed the door. The smell of tobacco on Bishop's jacket. The way the air hadn't quite settled down.

There were other flats in the house, though. Bishop didn't have to be out in the cold.

He checked that the crew weren't drawing attention to themselves, and had a final word.

"When I call, you get the van to the door. You understand what immediately means? Don't even answer. Just get the van to the door."

The way he'd work it, he decided, was not to make an attempt in the flat itself. Wait till Bettany was in, then get him coming back out, on the landing, on the stairs.

Not that this was set in stone. If you wanted a plan to work, you had to be ready to improvise.

He let himself into the house without bothering Greenfield. Upstairs, he spent ten minutes fiddling with the lock of the door opposite Liam Bettany's flat. Once he'd have been through it like butter, but his misspent youth was an ancient memory.

The flat was cold, but bearable. He checked it was empty, then dragged an armchair into the hallway. The front door had a peephole, and nobody was getting into Liam Bettany's place without Bishop knowing about it.

Take him on the landing, take him on the stairs. Quick zap of the stun gun and it was game over, right there.

But be ready to improvise, he warned himself.

He settled in to wait.

The man pushing the trays of croissants had disappeared through a shop doorway, but the fresh-baked smell lingered. Otherwise, it was the usual street odours—traffic and grime and old clothing.

Bettany said, "Keep walking."

She said, "Dear boy. Think about it. Why would I have someone killed in order to persuade you to kill someone else? Why wouldn't I just have had the someone else killed in the first place?"

Because you think in circles, Bettany thought. Because there was always the chance that this moment would happen, and this was always going to be your defence.

And because if you got me to do it, the link between yourself and the act would be invisible. Even I wouldn't know my true motive.

He took a breath. On these same streets, years ago, he'd daily moved among people who trafficked in weaponry that somewhere down the line would maim and kill innocents. Right now, he'd have preferred their company.

Stay on track, he thought. Follow this through to the end.

He said, "So what are you telling me? That it was actually Driscoll who killed him?"

"That would be neat, wouldn't it? Are you likely to believe me if I said that was so?"

"I doubt I'd believe you if you told me this was London."

"Harsh." She pursed her lips. "Well, then. No, Driscoll had nothing to do with Liam's death either. Though I confess I had hoped that ten minutes of Mr. Coe trying to convince you otherwise would persuade you that he had."

It went beyond arrogance. She viewed the world through a prism all her own, by the light of which things existed solely in relation to her.

Whoever had killed him, Liam had been her piece of Lego.

He said, "What was his motive supposed to be?"

"You've met Vincent."

"Yes."

"How hard would you have to look for a motive? Vincent is . . . askew."

Bettany said, "And you thought that would tip the balance for me? That Driscoll's a touch out there? That's evidence?"

"I confess, I'd thought you'd be a little less on your game. A little more raddled, after drinking your way round the rougher ports of Europe. No disrespect, dear, but wasn't that a touch retro?"

"I considered the French Foreign Legion," Bettany said. "But I didn't like their hats."

"There. A quip makes everything rosier, doesn't it?"

"You're very sure I won't kill you."

She gave him a motherly look. "Oh, you're not going to do that. You beat a man half to death once, didn't you? On the McGarrys' instructions. That was one of the reasons I thought you could be relied on to extract a proper vengeance. But killing me, here, now? There'd be no purpose. I did not harm your son."

"Somebody killed him."

"No."

"You had Kask do it."

"No. Your son fell."

And this time there was something in her eyes he hadn't seen there until now. This time, he thought, she was telling the truth.

"Your son fell," she said again, gently. "Nobody pushed him."

"He wasn't alone on that balcony—"

"A deduction based on the absence of matches or a lighter. I'm right, aren't I?"

He could almost see it come tumbling down, this house of cards he'd built. She knew. And there was only one way that was possible.

"Straight-line thinking, Mr. Bettany. It's an asset in a field operative. It prevents clouded judgement, allows you to plough on and get the job done. But it's not always—"

"What did you do?"

"A piece of evidence was removed. That's all."

It was Bettany's turn to come to a halt, suddenly enough that someone bumped into him. He turned, caught a glimpse of a grey hoodie.

Whoever it was bustled past, and was gone.

Tearney said, "There was a policeman."

"Welles," Bettany said.

He remembered Welles's helpfulness. Taking him to the crematorium, directing him to Liam's flat. Delivering Liam's effects.

Minus Liam's lighter.

"He was very useful last year," Dame Ingrid said. "After the unpleasantness with the, ah, gangbanger that Mr. Kask murdered. Policemen are so open to persuasion, don't you find?"

His mind was still reeling. He felt like he'd taken a blow to the head.

"He was quite happy to let Oskar have the lighter, not that anyone needed to have it. He could have simply disposed of it. But Oskar . . . Well. Oskar had his own way of doing things."

He said, "I spoke to Marten Saar. Oskar's blown. Did you know that?"

"I thought there was probably a reason his body turned up in a lift shaft."

She knew. He hadn't read a trace of it in her features, but that was another advantage to her Toby-mug face.

"An accident in the early hours," she said. "Apparently the doors opened at the wrong moment, and poor Oskar didn't look where he was stepping."

"So you lose," he said. "Both ways, you lose."

"Be careful, Mr. Bettany."

"Vincent's still alive, so your money's history. And your plan to infiltrate the local franchise of the Russian mafia's up in smoke too. Not a good day for your bank balance or your job."

"I'll survive."

"And that's it? You'll survive? The end?"

"What were you expecting? A desperate rage that you failed to play your part? Mr. Bettany, I run a very large, very busy Service. You have no idea how many schemes I've overseen that came to nothing. You get used to it."

"My son died," he said flatly. "And you used that for leverage. You used me."

"Your son was a loser, Mr. Bettany. A pothead and a loser. He fell off that balcony because he was stoned, and he was stoned because he was a loser. He only had a job because he got lucky on a computer game. You have to wonder, don't you, if he'd had a father around, would he have ended up that way? Please don't."

This, because his hand had gone to his pocket, and the heavy warm weight of the gun.

"Do you really think I make this journey alone every day? Even if I wanted to, they wouldn't let me."

His hand stayed where it was.

"The last thing you'll know," she said, "is me tugging my earlobe."

"And what if you're bluffing?"

"There's only one way to find out. That's why they call it bluffing."

He didn't look around. It made sense that she would have people watching her, but he found he didn't care one way or the other. What mattered more was that he believed her about Liam, that there had been no murder, and that his son's death was nothing more than a druggy accident. But for all that, she'd used Liam's death as if it were of no more consequence than a broken bottle.

The ends she'd sought, he didn't much care about. But the means she'd chosen—for that, he thought, he could kill her.

Perhaps she sensed this, because something in her gaze wavered.

She said, "You do realise that if you do anything foolish, the consequences will be . . . severe."

"You think I care?"

"About yourself, perhaps not. But there are protocols. If you produce that gun, there'll be repercussions beyond your own death."

"I have no family."

"And no one you care about."

"No."

"Then it won't disturb you to know that anyone you've had contact with since your return to this country will come to harm."

He almost laughed. "Dancer Blaine? Marten Saar?"

"I was thinking of Felicity Pointer."

He closed his mouth.

"And Driscoll, and that man of his. And Mr. Coe, of course. Possibly others. Are you prepared to have their deaths on your conscience?"

"That wouldn't happen."

"The attempted murder of the head of the Intelligence

Service, Mr. Bettany? There'll be official inquiries, yes. But there'll also be payback."

He stared into her eyes, and saw no sign that she was bluffing.

They were drawing glances now. Standing on this street, in this busy corner of London. Electricity coming off them, probably.

She said, "So what happens next is simple. You return to the life you were, until recently, squandering in the great ports of Europe, and it'll be like this never happened."

"Meaning you'll find some other way of dealing with Driscoll."

"That would be foolish of me, given what you know. No, Mr. Driscoll will remain unharmed, as will Ms. Pointer and everyone else."

This with the air of a fairy godmother, waving her wand and promising future happiness.

"My own difficulties will, I'm sure, prove soluble by other means. You didn't think yours was the only iron in my fire, did you?"

He said, "And I walk away unharmed."

"You have my word."

No expression crossed his face. It didn't have to.

She said, "In the circumstances, I'm not likely to put it in writing. But dealing with you would be an added complication. And it's not like any of this is on the books."

For a long moment, Bettany said nothing. His hand remained inside his jacket, resting on the handle of the Makarov.

Dame Ingrid raised her own hand. Let her fingers rest on her little slab of a chin.

"One tug on an earlobe," she said.

"It would be so easy," he replied, but didn't finish the sentence. She knew.

He turned and walked away.

5.10

ngrid Tearney watched him go. So this was how a field agent felt. Her heart rate had climbed new heights in the past thirty minutes. For half a moment there, right at the end, she'd thought he was going to kill her.

And the reason he hadn't, she decided, had nothing to do with her threats of instant reprisal—a tug on her earlobe, an armed response from her security detail. It was the thought of what would follow, the deaths of the others involved.

As it happened, she'd been lying about the security detail, and the widespread slaughter of civilians didn't feature among the protocols that would follow the murder of the head of the Intelligence Service.

Joes thought a life spent in committee rooms left you soft. But it had taught her to lie like a bastard.

Useful skill.

She reached for her phone now, reflecting on another of her recent lies, that it would be possible for Bettany to return to his old life. Of course, he almost certainly didn't believe that either.

He had to know that he knew too much. Besides, he had seen her fear, and she really couldn't allow that.

The number she sought was near the top of her call list.

There was no Oskar to instruct any more. A pity, because a line into the Cousins' Circle would have been a professional triumph, but hardly a tragedy. Oskar Kask, her wholly-owned gangster, had been malleable, conscienceless, but incapable of subtlety. A blunt object. And since he'd proved not blunt enough to deal with Bettany yesterday, he'd not have been much use to her even if he weren't dead today.

She called the number.

"Ma'am?"

"I have a name. Majeed Ansari."

There was a pause, the suggestion of fingers rattling on a keyboard.

"He's Priority Scott, Ma'am."

Level one—she knew he was. She'd put him there herself before her first conversation with JK Coe. *Majeed Ansari* was a name that easily lent itself to such a list, readily suggesting that its owner might harbour dangerous, violent ideals.

As far as Tearney was aware, Majeed Ansari had as many terrorist sympathies as a tortoise, but it was the name that counted.

"I'm hearing rumours," she said. "Check him for contact with former Service personnel."

She killed the call.

So where am I now, wondered Bettany?

Adrift again was where.

He'd spent the best part of a decade taking the Brothers McGarry off the board only to find that others had filled the gap. The world might technically be a safer place, but you'd need pretty sophisticated measuring equipment to be sure. It was the same with Dame Ingrid. Any vacancy she left would have been sealed within hours, another Dame Ingrid springing up like a skeleton warrior sown from teeth. He'd have gained half a moment's victory before he was dead too, but there'd be no coming back for him. He'd scattered teeth in his time, but they'd fallen on stony ground.

Besides, in the moment he'd come closest to violence, he'd seen the fear in her eyes.

If he'd killed her, and walked away—if she'd been bluffing about her security cover—he'd have had to live with himself afterwards. And she was right, he was no murderer. Witnessing her fear had confirmed that. A monster she might be, scheming away in a labyrinth of her own making, but she was a human being too. Liam wouldn't have wanted him to kill her. He felt sure of that, on no evidence whatever. Liam would not have wanted the use she'd made of his death to be the reason for her own.

And a line came to him, he didn't know from where, about snow falling on everyone, like the descent of their last end. On all the living and the dead.

Enough. London wasn't safe, and he needed to leave. But first he had more scattering to deal with.

Not teeth but ashes.

Tearney's phone rang.

She was back in her own world, where the pedestrians were purposeful and the traffic expensive. Big trees scratched each other overhead. *Bare ruined choirs . . .*

"Yes."

"We've a positive on your rumour."

A positive on your rumour. Once upon a time, everyone who spoke English spoke English.

"And?"

"A former agent, Thomas Bettany. Associate, friend and co-worker of Majeed Ansari's in Marseilles, where Ansari's lived since '08."

Tearney sighed, and allowed the sound to carry through her phone.

Where late the sweet birds sang.

A former Service agent, consorting with a suspected terrorist. It didn't look good for Bettany.

Of course, it had helped that Ansari had the right sort of ethnic profile, but if it hadn't been that, it would have been something else. No one ever accused Dame Ingrid of lacking resource.

"Bettany's current whereabouts—"

"He's in London," Dame Ingrid said.

She gave them Liam Bettany's address.

"Take him there. In the flat."

"On what footing?"

She was outside her own building. Regent's Park. The pinnacle of her professional ambition, and launching pad for her myth. No, she'd never been a field agent, but the thing about joes was, they lived and died in the shadows, where they belonged. Once they were gone, their final identities chiselled on headstones, their sins and victories vanished with them. Whereas Dame Ingrid—never a joe—would forever be part of the recorded history of the Service.

Obviously she'd be first to honour their memory, but the simple truth was, she was worth more than them. Her name would live in the history books, and theirs, only in the bowels of the building in front of her. It was fitting that her lifestyle reflect this. It wasn't about greed. It was about what was appropriate.

"Ma'am?"

"Waterproof," she said. "The footing is Code Waterproof."

She ended the call, and entered the building, to continue her work.

Dry-cleaning, they called it. The process by which you made sure you had no tail. So Bettany led nobody a merry dance, because nobody was following him. Perhaps Tearney had shadows for her morning commute, but if so they'd stuck with her when he'd cut loose. So the doubling back along busy streets, and the underground games, nipping across platforms to jump a train heading back in the opposite direction, were all without point, if tradecraft was ever without point. He thought he'd know if he was being followed, but that in itself was dangerous, the confidence in his own senses. Trust but verify. The dry-cleaning had verified.

In a churchyard near Liam's he sat on a bench in the cold. A pair of magpies were squabbling among headstones. For a moment he couldn't remember the rhyme, what two magpies signified, and when he did he wasn't convinced.

The descent of their last end . . .

He could leave now, and avoid the flat altogether. It would be the sensible thing to do. Forget the ashes, forget Liam. Walk away.

But nobody walks. He'd tried that before.

After a while in which nothing happened—no new thoughts startled him, no sudden sounds—he got to his feet. The magpies flew away.

In the flat, he went straight to the kitchen. The urn containing Liam's ashes were on the table, and he was reaching for it when something hit him between the shoulderblades. For one brief moment he was a light switch someone was turning on. He had the faintest sensation of causing something to fall but it was too intangible to create a memory. When he woke, nothing remained of it.

He was on his side in a moving vehicle, wrists and ankles bound, a sack over his head.

For the first few minutes a slow accretion of detail occupied him. That the vehicle ran smoothly. That it was a van of some sort. That through the sack he could make out no light, so its windows were presumably blanked out ...

That there was at least one other person with him, though for the moment they remained silent.

About to speak, he changed his mind. Once he spoke, once they answered, a question would be resolved. He would know whether they'd come for Tom Bettany or Martin Boyd, whether it was a team sent by Ingrid Tearney, in which case his future was bleak, or whether the Brothers McGarry's crew had found him, in which case it was bleaker.

Some things, he could wait to find out. Soon, he would know who he was at this moment.

Closing his eyes, he listened to the beating of his heart.

PART SIX

■ ■ ■

6

It was two days later that Flea Pointer came by the flat, partly because she wondered what had become of Bettany, but partly because she'd left a book there once, and was hoping to retrieve it.

Life at Lunchbox was changing. Vincent, in the grip of a new idea, had arranged whiteboards around the office, on which everyone had been invited to scribble. The central character would be the target of dark conspiracies, the specific nature of which was left to be determined by the player. It would be less about unleashing the hero within, he said, and more about allowing the inner paranoiac free rein. His eyes had stayed bright while he'd said this.

The previous version of *Shades 3* would be scrapped. The new one would be a serious proposition, maybe a money-maker. Things, Vincent said, would be different.

Flea had the sense he meant more than just the game.

The landlord made little fuss about letting her into the flat, seeming resigned to such intrusions. "It all stops Wednesday," he said, meaning that's when the rent ran out. But everything had stopped some time ago, where Liam was concerned. Flea was dismayed at how swiftly the place had become abandoned. A faint chemical tang stained the air, but that apart, there was nothing to suggest Tom Bettany's recent presence, or not until she went into the kitchen.

For there, on the floor, she found the urn containing Liam's ashes, lid askew. And Liam himself . . . what remained of Liam was a thin drift across the lino, like something you'd get if you dropped a dustpan.

For a long while Flea stood in the doorway, leaning against the jamb. It was very quiet. At length, when she could bear it no more, she found a brush in the cupboard beneath the sink, and did what she could to make things right again.

ACKNOWLEDGMENTS

For advice, support, encouragement and friendship, I'm more than grateful to:

Bronwen Hruska and her team at Soho Press, especially Paul Oliver, Rudy Martinez, Amara Hoshijo and the unflappable Juliet Grames;

Juliet Burton and Micheline Steinberg;

Cara Black, Jim Benn, Henry Chang and Lisa Brackmann;

Tony Smith and Christine Delaney;

Adam, Tom and Kat;

and Chris, Nick and Jo.